THE BLOOMSBURY GROUP

Henrietta's War by Joyce Dennys
The Brontës Went to Woolworths by Rachel Ferguson
Miss Hargreaves by Frank Baker
Love's Shadow by Ada Leverson
Mrs Tim of the Regiment by D.E. Stevenson

A NOTE ON THE AUTHOR

WOLF MANKOWITZ was born in 1924 on Fashion Street in Spitalfields in London's East End, the heart of London's Jewish community, where his father was a bookseller in the streetmarkets. This background provided him with the material for three famous novels, *A Kid for Two Farthings, Make Me An Offer* and *My Old Man's a Dustman. Make Me An Offer* was adapted for film in 1954 and *A Kid for Two Farthings* was adapted the following year by the director Carol Reed. In 1958 he wrote the book for the hit West End musical *Expresso Bongo*, later made into a film starring Cliff Richard.

Mankowitz's remarkable output has included novels, plays, historical studies and the screenplays for many successful films that have received awards, including the Oscar for *The Bespoke Overcoat*, a BAFTA for the screenplay of *The Day the Earth Caught Fire*, and the Cannes Grand Prix for *The Hireling*.

In 1962, Mankowitz offered to introduce friend Cubby Broccoli and Harry Saltzman, holder of the film rights to James Bond, when Broccoli mentioned he desired to make the Bond series his next film project. The two men formed a partnership and began co-producing the first Bond film, *Doctor No*, for which Mankowitz was hired as one of the screenwriters. He later also collaborated on the screenplay for *Casino Royale*. Mankowitz died in 1998, in County Cork, Ireland. His ashes are at the Golders Green Crematorium.

Published by Bloomsbury USA, New York

ISBN 978-1-60819-048-5

First published in 1953 by Andre Deutsch Ltd
This paperback edition published in 2010 by Bloomsbury USA

10 9 8 7 6 5 4 3 2 1

Typeset by Macmillan Publishing Solutions
Printed in the United States of America by Quebecor World Fairfield

A Kid for Two Farthings

A Novel

Wolf Mankowitz

NEW YORK · BERLIN · LONDON

For My Grandfather and His
Great-Grandsons

IT was thanks to Mr Kandinsky that Joe knew a unicorn when he saw one.

He also knew that the Elephant and Castle was the In-fanta of Castile, a Spanish princess. He knew that Moses was an Egyptian priest, that the Chinese invented fire-works, that Trotsky was the best revolutionary, and that pregnant was going to have a baby. Joe was six, and thanks to Mr Kandinsky, he was educated, although he didn't go to school, for he had to look after his mother till they came to Africa.

His father said to Joe when he was still five, 'Look after Mother till you come,' and Joe said he would. Then he went down to talk to Mr Kandinsky in the basement. No teacher knew what Mr Kandinsky knew, about the Elephant and Castle, that is, and the unicorn. Soon after,

Joe's father went to Africa, with two suitcases and a Madeira hat for the hot weather.

Joe lived upstairs at number III Fashion Street. There was a bedroom and a kitchen, and the kitchen had a fire-place and a gas stove, but no sink. The tap was at the top of the first flight of stairs, and Mr Kandinsky used it, too. The lavatory was in the yard at the back and smelt of Keating's Powder. Mr Kandinsky lived in a room on the ground floor, and had a workshop in the basement. The workshop had a window below ground level, and there was an iron grille over the pavement for the light to come through. In the little area outside the window were bits of newspaper and an old hat and a sauce bottle, and Joe wondered how they got through the iron bars, because it was a top hat and the bottle was the tomato-sauce kind with a wide bottom.

'We ought to look, Mr Kandinsky,' Joe said one day, 'because maybe there are some pound notes and six-pences mixed up with it all.'

'Joe,' replied Mr Kandinsky, 'who has pound notes or even sixpences to lose in Fashion Street?'

So the window was never open, except in the summer it was lowered a few inches at the top, and a lot of dust came into the workshop.

Mr Kandinsky was a trousers-maker. In the workshop he had a sewing-machine, and a bench with the surface all shining from where he and

Shmule pressed the trousers. In the fireplace were two big gas-rings with two big goose-irons beside them. When the cloth was soaked in a pail and spread over the trousers, and the hot goose-iron pressed on top, a great cloud of steam arose. Mr Kandinsky always said it was bad for your health and the worst thing in the tailoring, even bringing on the consumption. On the wall were three hooks with large brown-paper and card-board patterns hanging on them. On the mantel were two boxes with flat pieces of white tailors' chalks in them, and hundreds of cloth patterns in books, and dozens of reels of cotton.

Mr Kandinsky had two pictures. Over his bench was a big print of a lady with her head bowed sitting on top of a large grey-green ball. Her eyes were bandaged and she was holding a broken harp. Joe thought the lady was a street musician who had been in a car accident; she was crying because her harp was broken and she couldn't live by singing any more. Mr Kandinsky looked at the picture for a while and said, 'You know, Joe, maybe you're right. But what about the ball she is sitting on?'

Joe thought it over while Mr Kandinsky hand-stitched a pair of fine worsted trousers, but in the end he had to give up. Then Mr Kandinsky told him:

'This ball is the world and this lady is Hope who is always with the world. She is blindfold because if she could see what happens she would lose hope and then where would she be? What this broken harp means, I don't know.'

'Maybe it's a bit of another painting,' Joe said.

'Maybe it is,' said Mr Kandinsky. 'Who knows?'

'Who knows?' repeated Joe, because he liked the way Mr Kandinsky said things. 'Who knows?' he said again, putting his head to one side, opening his hands and trying to lift his eyebrows.

The other picture was a brown photograph of an old man with a long beard and side curls, and bushy eye-brows, and a great curved nose with curved nostrils. This was Mr Kandinsky's father. 'A pious man, Joe,' Mr Kandinsky said, 'very respected in the village, the finest coat-maker in the whole country.'

'Not a trousers-maker?' asked Joe.

'Certainly not,' said Mr Kandinsky. 'He was a great man, and he would never lower himself to be a trousers-maker.'

'Why aren't you a coat-maker, Mr Kandinsky?' asked Joe.

Mr Kandinsky, who could answer all questions, replied, 'Because my wise father put me to trousers-making, thinking that Kandinsky and Son would be able to make complete suits. And you know what that means, Joe? It means bespoke tailoring - no more jobbing for other people. You can be an artist, not just a workman; some-body can send you sackcloth and you will make it up into a pair of trousers. But it was not to be. It was a dream, Joe. Never mind. Life is all dreams - dreams and work. That's all it is.'

After this talk, Joe nodded at the photograph of Reb Zadek Kandinsky when he came into the workshop. The stern eyes looked past him into the future, a lost future of Kandinsky and Son, bespoke tailors. The curved nostrils turned disdainfully away from Mr Kandinsky, the Fashion Street trousers-maker, well known in the trade, but not in the same class as his father, a master-tailor, who died cross-legged on his bench, stitching the reveres of the first coat he made in London. 'May he find his place in peace,' Mr Kandinsky said. 'That last coat was beautiful, I tell you, Joe, beautiful.'

'I think your trousers are lovely, Mr Kandinsky,' Joe said, to cheer Mr Kandinsky up.

'Thank you, Joe,' he answered. 'I will make you a pair of blue serge trousers.' And he did, a real pair of trousers with turn-ups, and a cash pocket. Everything, even proper flies.

The whole house was Mr Kandinsky's, not his, but he paid the whole rent and Joe's mother gave him ten shillings every week. He was an old friend and the arrangement was made before Joe's father went away. Mr Kandinsky could spare the room. 'I am the only Kandinsky extant - which means the last Kandinsky,' he told Joe. Joe thought how it must make you old to be the last one extant. He looked at Mr Kandinsky. He was very old, but his face wasn't worn out. In fact he had much more face than Joe, and Joe wasn't extant at all, having both his mother and father as well as Mr Kandinsky. Joe kept a pet in the backyard, a day-old chick, which sometimes lived for two or three weeks. After Mr Kandinsky told him he had no people he called his pets Kandinsky in memory of that family.

At Friday night supper Mr Kandinsky and Joe's mother talked about Africa and Joe's father and what he was doing there and how soon Joe and his mother would go out to him.

'You know, Rebecca,' Mr Kandinsky said, 'your fried fish is not just fish – it is manna from heaven.'

'You are always paying me compliments, Mr Kandinsky,' Joe's mother said.

'And why not, Rebecca?' said Mr Kandinsky. 'You are the prettiest girl in the whole East End.'

'Girl,' said Joe's mother, and laughed, blushing so that she did indeed look quite pretty.

'Isn't she pretty, Joe?' asked Mr Kandinsky.

'I think you are very pretty and nice,' Joe said to his mother, although she had stopped smiling, and her face looked sad and not so pretty.

'For how long?' she said. 'How long is anyone pretty?' Mr Kandinsky cleared his throat, which meant he was going to say something important. Joe looked at him, waiting.

'You are pretty as long as someone loves you, Rebecca,' he said, 'and so many people love you that, believe me, you are very pretty. Look at me. I am ugly, and old, but even I am pretty when someone loves me.'

'I love you, Mr Kandinsky,' Joe said. 'One morning you will look quite pretty.' Mr Kandinsky put his hand on Joe's head.

'Thank you, Joe,' he said. 'I feel a little prettier already. To celebrate I will have one more piece of this wonderful fish which the miracle of your mother's cooking has made as sweet as honey.' Mr Kandinsky, Joe thought, never got tired of fried fish.

'So what does he say in his letter this week?' Mr Kandinsky would ask. 'How is the Kaffir business?'

Joe's mother read parts of the letter out aloud, with Mr Kandinsky stopping her every so often by raising his hand and asking a question. Then they would discuss the matter for a few minutes before she went on reading. Sometimes they were very long letters, full of business details, five gross of stewards' jackets, twenty gross denim trousers, add ten per cent for carriage costs, a hundred-pound company, five pounds paid up, salesman's commission on a hundred ex-army bell tents, and so on.

These letters were full of excitement, with little stories of Kaffirs drinking their white beer and
singing, or Kaffir boys met late at night march-
ing down the street beating a drum, and Joe's
father walking in the road, otherwise they would
beat him up. The long excited letters had money
in them. As Rebecca opened them, the corner of
a five-pound note, and once a ten-pound note,
and always a few pounds, would be seen. Unusual,
exciting notes they were; not ordinary, but
African money. But other letters were very short.
There was no message in them for Joe or
Mr Kandinsky at all, and for Rebecca just a few
words. These were the bad letters, and if Joe
asked too many questions after they arrived, his
mother's face would look at him as if she couldn't
see, and if he went on asking questions, it would
suddenly begin to tremble and then she would
cry, hugging him and making his face wet with
her tears.

In the mornings Joe's mother went to the
Whitechapel Road, where she worked in a
millinery shop. She trimmed hats with bunches of
artificial fruit and flowers, and Mr Kandinsky said
she was the best and most artistic hattrimmer in
the millinery trade. Because she didn't come
home until the late afternoon, Joe ate with Mr
Kandinsky and Shmule at twelve o'clock, downstairs, in the workshop. Mr Kandinsky never

allowed Joe's mother to leave something cooked for them.

'I am an old cook myself,' he told Joe; 'although your mother is the best cook in the world, Joe - I am not saying anything against her cooking.'

Mr Kandinsky cooked on one of the gas-rings in the workshop. On one of them a big goose-iron was always heating, and on the other a large cooking-pot with two handles bubbled quietly all morning long. Into the pot Mr Kandinsky threw pieces of beef or a small breast of lamb, with plenty of onions and pepper and salt, and some large potatoes. Or a large marrow bone cooked with carrots, or mutton cooked with haricot beans. At quarter to twelve Joe went up the street to the baker on the corner to buy three onion-rolls. Then they all sat down with big enamel plates full of steaming stew, eating and talking. Joe liked Mr Kandinsky's cooking very much. 'The best cooks are men, Joe,' said Mr Kandinsky. 'Some men cooks get thousands of pounds from the Kings of Europe for cooking dinners no better than this.'

Mr Kandinsky talked a lot, but Shmule was often quiet. Shmule was short and broad, and very strong. He had bright red hair which curled into small flames, although after a haircut it was more like a piece of astrakhan. His skin was pale and his eyes grey, and every Saturday he spent the whole day at the gymnasium developing himself. Developing yourself was the only thing Shmule wanted to talk about, which was the reason why he said very little, because Joe was too young to develop himself much, and Mr Kandinsky was already too old. Occasionally Mr Kandinsky would bring Shmule into the conversation by saying, 'You got a new muscle to show us?'

Shmule at once took off his jacket. He rolled up his shirt sleeves and clenched his fists and bent his elbows till large knots appeared everywhere. Sometimes he took his shirt off as well. He put his arms over his head, and enormous bands of muscle stood up on his back and chest. Joe clapped and Mr Kandinsky called Shmule 'Maccabaeus', which means 'The Hammer', and was the name in which Shmule wrestled. But once or twice Shmule tried a new muscle, and though it came up a little distance it fell down straight away. Then he blushed from his forehead to his neck, and went into a corner to practise.

Shmule was going to be a wrestling champion, which meant he had to beat Louis Dalmatian, the Stepney Thrasher, Turk Robert, Bully Bason, and the dreaded Python Macklin. He didn't have to beat them all at once, but even one at a time was enough, especially the dreaded Python Macklin, who had broken limbs with his powerful scissors grip. Shmule showed them the scissors.

He took a chair and fought with it on the floor, twining his legs round it and pressing hard, explaining all the while, until one of the chair legs cracked and Mr Kandinsky shouted, 'The furniture he breaks up!'

'A chair I can mend,' said Shmule, puffing and blowing, 'but supposing it was my leg?'

So between Shmule and Mr Kandinsky, Joe learnt a great deal about the world. Though he was a bit young, Shmule taught him the position of defence and how to give an uppercut. But it was Mr Kandinsky who told Joe all about unicorns.

It was the afternoon that Joe's chick Kandinsky was found dead on its back, legs in the air, a ball of cotton wool and two matchsticks. Joe was worried because he did everything the day-old chick man in Club Row told him to do, and yet the chick died. Mr Kandinsky suggested that perhaps it could happen that Joe wasn't a natural-born chicken-raiser. Chickens just weren't his speciality. Maybe he should try a dog or a lizard, or a couple of fish. This made Joe think why not write to his father for a big animal, because naturally small animals only have small lives and naturally they lose them more easily.

Mr Kandinsky had been studying Africa in some detail since Joe's father went there, but the parts in the book about the gold mines and diamond mines were not as interesting as the chapter called the Fauna of Central Africa. He was, consequently, in an excellent position to advise Joe on the habits of larger animals.

They discussed the lion with some hope, because many cubs have been trained into good pets, but lions only eat meat, and where would they get enough to feed it? You couldn't fool a lion with vegetable stew; even Mr Kandinsky's cooking would only make it angry, and then there would be trouble. The giraffe was nice, but with such a long neck, you couldn't get it in the house. A zebra is only a horse with stripes, and horses you can see any day in the street.

'Maybe,' Joe suggested, 'maybe my father could send a unicorn.'

'A unicorn is a public-house,' Shmule said, looking up from a small book he was reading, *The Principles of Judo*.

'Don't show your ignorance on the subject, Shmule,' Mr Kandinsky said. Then he told Joe about unicorns.

'Every animal when it was made by the Almighty was given one extra-special present,' said Mr Kandinsky. 'The squirrel was given a wonderful tail to hold on with so he wouldn't fall from the trees; the horse was given strong fine legs so he could run fast; the lion great jaws; the elephant a trunk so he could take a shower whenever he felt like it, because an elephant is so large, how else could he keep clean? But the unicorn got the most special present of all. He was given a magic horn which could cure anything anyone was ever sick from. It could grant anybody's wish - straight off. And this horn consequently was worth £10,000 cash on sight, anywhere in the world. Don't ask me why the unicorn got this present. Someone had to get it, so why not him? Anyhow, he got it and no one else. But because of this very gift unicorns became so scarce you won't even find one in the zoo, so it is in life.

'At one time unicorns were common as cart-horses: wherever you went in the streets you would see half a dozen. In those days no one was poor. You needed something, so, all right, you just reached out your hand and there it was: a glass of lemon tea, a new hat. Then, when people became poor, all the unicorns had their horns stolen and sold. You can imagine what that did to them. Could a lion live without his jaws, could a squirrel swing from the trees without his tail, could an elephant go on without a shower-bath, could I eat if I stopped making trousers? Of course not. So how could a unicorn live without his horn?

'Ah, Joe, they died in their thousands, the lovely unicorns. They gathered together in dusty yards and at the bottom of those streets which lead nowhere. They nuzzled one another for comfort, and closed their eyes so as not to be reminded of what they had lost. Their fine white coats became spotted, their beautiful sleek muscles slipped away into twisted sinew. They pined, they shrank, they faded, they died, and their death was sad, for they had been eaten up by poverty, swallowed in the darkness of a pit with no bottom, so that no one ever saw them again.'

Mr Kandinsky sighed as he bent to throw his cold goose-iron on to the gas-ring. He looked at Joe with big eyes and sighed. 'This was the pity of it, my Joe,' he said. 'The unicorns passed away, but poverty was still in the world, poverty and sickness. Strong men have wasted away, beautiful girls have grown ugly, children have been lost before they could yet walk, the unicorns are all gone and yet poverty is still here. Don't ask me why. What do I know?' He sighed again, then put his hand on Joe's shoulder, pressing so as to feel the small fine bone. 'Never mind,' he said. 'Sometimes, in spite of everything, a child grows well, a man goes from strength to strength, a woman's face does not fade. In the same way some unicorns must have lived. They were the clever ones. They saw how things were going and didn't waste time blaming men or cursing life, or threatening God, or any other foolishness. Instead they came forward and said to the rest,

"Listen, friends. If we don't do something soon there will be no unicorns left in the world."

' "Be quiet," some of them shouted. "Can't you see we are too unhappy to do anything?" '

' "Don't be blasphemous," others cried. "It's the will of God." '

' "Don't interrupt us when we are crying," others said. "It is the only thing left for us to enjoy." '

'But some gathered together to escape, some with hope in their hearts, some with doubt, a few with the spirit which does not care either for hope or doubt. These said, "Living means waste, but let who wants to live, live." '

'One old unicorn who had been told about Africa when he was a baby had never forgotten. He told them, and to Africa they went that very night. In Africa they are today, although their terrible experiences made them careful about being seen by men, so that nowadays you don't see them so often. But they are even bigger now, and stronger even, and so fierce they fight at the drop of a hat. Without doubt, Joe,' said Mr Kandinsky, 'without doubt, Shmule, you wrestler,' he said, 'there is absolutely no reason why there shouldn't be unicorns in Africa.'

'What do I know?' asked Shmule.

'Could you get a unicorn into the house?' Joe asked.

'A small unicorn,' Mr Kandinsky said, 'certainly. There is no reason why a small unicorn couldn't be got into the house. Would you like another spoonful, Joe?' He stirred the carrots in the saucepan on his gas-ring so that a great cloud arose.

AFTER Kandinsky the day-old chick died, Joe
went to the animal market, because if you
wanted a unicorn the best place in the world to
look for it was Club Row.

Joe had his own way of walking through the
market. It made it much larger if you started in
the middle where the herring-women fished
salted herrings out of barrels with red hands,
dipped them in water and cleaned and sliced them
thinly with long thin knives. From there you
walked up to Alf, the singing-bird man, then cut
round the back, coming through to the other end
where the dogs were. But if there was something
you wanted to buy it was much better to start at
one end by the singing birds and walk through,
looking carefully at every stall.

Alf, the singing-bird man, came to Mr
Kandinsky for repairs, so he knew Joe and always

spoke to him, even if he was busy selling someone
a canary. Alf was against day-old chicks as pets.
He pulled his light brown overall coat down,
pushed his cap back from his eyes and told Joe
when he bought Kandinsky, 'You ain't doing that
chick no favour, Joe, taking him away without his
mother, alone; he doesn't know how to give a
peep-peep yet; putting him in a box with a drop
of water and a handful of straw. That rotten day-
old chick man should be put in a box himself, the
louse, selling chicks to anyone with a sixpence. A
chick like this needs his mum or a special hot-box;
he don't just grow up any old how any old where;
he must have special care; he shouldn't catch cold.'
Alf turned to a fat lady with a big grey fur round
her neck. 'That canary, lady,' he said, 'is such
a singer I should like to see better.'

'He don't appear to be singing much just now,'
the lady said, taking a handful of potato-crisps
from a bag and crunching them. 'Tweet-tweet,'
she said to the canary, spitting a few little bits of
potato-crisp at him, 'tweet-tweet.'

'Here, Oscar,' Alf said, because all his birds were
sold with their right names on small red certificates.
He whistled softly to the bird. Oscar turned his bead
eyes towards Alf, listened for a moment, and then
began to sing.

'Lovely,' the fat lady said, finishing the crisps
and brushing her fur. 'How much for the bird?'

'That Oscar,' Alf said afterwards, 'I had him nearly a year.' And he started to whistle softly to a dark gold canary.

Near Alf's stall there was a jellied-eel stand with a big enamel bowl of grey jellied eels, small bowls for portions, a large pile of lumps of bread, and three bottles of vinegar. There were also orange-and-black winkles in little tubs, and large pink whelks. People stood around shaking vinegar on to their eels and scooping them up with bread. A little thin man in a white muffler served them and sometimes dropped a large piece of eel on the ground. Behind the stand a very fat man with a striped apron and an Anthony Eden hat waved a ladle in his hand and shouted, 'Best eels, fresh jellied; buy 'em and try 'em.' Over the stand a red, white and blue banner flapped. 'The Eel King', it said. The King himself never served.

Opposite the Eel King was a red barrow with dark green water-melons, and a white enamel table-top with halves and slices of melon and a large knife. Joe pretended he couldn't make up his mind whether to buy some jellied eels or a slice of melon. He watched people eating eels and shaking vinegar on them, and then looked back at the large wide slices of red melon with glossy black seeds bursting from them.

In the end he bought a twopenny slice of melon and pretended it was jellied eels, scooping the red flesh with his teeth and saying 'Blast' and 'Bloody' when the seeds dropped to the pavement. Some of the seeds he saved so that when they were dry he could crack them between his teeth and get the thin nuts inside.

While he scraped the thick skin of the melon, Joe watched the Indian fortune-teller who wore a turban and sold green, yellow and red perfume in small bottles. Whenever a woman bought a bottle of perfume the Indian looked at her strangely. 'A little moment, dear lady', he said, 'a little moment while I look into the bowl.' He looked darkly into a large glass bowl which turned purple or orange, and sliding his hand beneath brought out a small envelope with a fortune in it; the pavement all round his stall was covered with torn envelopes. Once, when the market finished, Joe kicked his way through empty boxes and newspapers past the Indian's stall. He saw him counting sixpences into piles, and putting them into small blue bags, but the bowl looked like an ordinary bowl for gold-fish. An Indian girl who wore a long blue silk robe was packing the bottles into boxes on a barrow. When the Indian pushed the barrow away, the girl walked behind him; they went to the bottom of the street and turned away into the darkness under the railway arches, back to India.

The Sunday came when Joe had saved enough of the sixpences Mr Kandinsky gave him every week for helping in the workshop, to buy a unicorn, should one appear. Mr Kandinsky was always busy on Sunday mornings, and he hardly noticed Joe leave. He was arguing with a customer who wanted a zip fastener on his trousers, something to which Mr Kandinsky could not agree.

Joe ran quickly through the crowd to the singing-bird end of the market. Alf was talking to a budgerigar and a tall thin man with a sad face. The bird wasn't replying, but every so often the thin man said, 'It's no good, Alf - it's no good,' till at last Alf put the cage down. Then the bird suddenly said, 'Hello', and Joe said hello back. The thin man looked sadder still and left, and Alf said, 'Talks better English than I do. Hello, Joe, what are you after? No more chicks, remember.'

'Do you know where I can find a unicorn, Alf?' Joe asked.

'Try down by the dogs, Joe,' Alf suggested. 'Hello,' the bird said again.

'Hello,' Joe replied and started towards the other end of the market.

On the way Mrs Quinn, the hen woman, called him over.

'Joe,' she said, 'tell your mother I'll bring the eggs over meself tomorrow.' She was holding a fat hen which squawked as an old woman pinched it and complained. 'If you don't like the bird, for the love of St Patrick leave it,' shouted

Mrs Quinn in Yiddish. 'So tell your mother now,' she said to Joe.

'Do you know where I can buy a unicorn, Mrs Quinn?' Joe asked.

'What do you want with heathen animals?' she answered. 'Get yourself a nice day-old chick.'

'That day-old chick man, the louse,' Joe said, 'he should be put in a box.'

'Will you leave the bird alone now?' screamed Mrs Quinn at the old woman, who was still pinching its bottom.

'There's no harm,' Joe thought, 'in at least having a look at the chicks.'

At the stall, hundreds of them were running about in a large glass enclosure with a paraffin lamp in the middle of it, all squeaking like mice. When someone bought them they were put into cardboard boxes with air-holes, and the squeaking became fainter. It was a pity they had such small lives.

'Another one already, cock?' asked the chick man.

'Not today, thank you,' said Joe. 'I'm not a born chick-raiser.'

'You got to know the trick of it, cock.'

'I'm going to buy a unicorn this time,' Joe said.

'You do that,' the man said, 'you do that.' He bundled two dozen chicks into a box and tied it up with string.

Just about the middle of the market, near the herring women, was the fritter stall which also sold hokey-pokey ices and sarsaparilla fancy drinks. The smell rushed up so thick from the great vat of frying oil that if you stood nearby for a while you had a whole meal of fritters. The hokey-pokey man called out, 'Get your hokey-pokey, penny a lump, the more you eat the more you jump,' but Joe hurried on. He passed the cat-lady with her basket of kittens mewing, and the long line of hutches where the rabbits were always eating. He waited for the bearded sandwich-board man to shout at him, 'The wages of sin is death, repent lest ye perish,' because he was studying to spit when he spoke. 'Sthin - death,' Joe spluttered as he hurried on.

The dog-sellers mostly stood in the gutter or against the bill-hoardings holding a puppy in each hand and one in each pocket. They didn't say anything unless you patted a pup. Then they told you he was a pedigree Irish retrieving elk-hound, his mother was a good house dog. A few of them had cages with bigger dogs in them, and one or two men just stood around with four or five dogs on leads, trying to make them stop walking round in circles and jumping at people. There were dogs with short legs and long tails, and dogs with short tails but long ears. They were all dogs all right, all yelping and barking, just dogs.

Joe walked right to the end of the dog-end of the market, hurrying past the man who bit off exactly at the joint dogs' tails that needed lopping, to the very last man standing by the arches under the railway. The four sixpences and four pennies in his pocket clinked and three men tried to sell him pedigreed pups, but the last man stood by the dark opening of the arches without speaking. He held a large white rabbit under one arm, and in the other hand a piece of tattered string, and at the end of the string, a small unicorn.

While Joe looked at the unicorn, a little man with three pullovers on came up and took the white rabbit. He held it up by its ears, and it kicked its feet at him. Then he handed it back, saying, 'Flemish?'

'Dutch,' the last man said.

'Thought it was Flemish,' the little man mumbled as he turned away.

'Dutch,' the man said again.

'Funny thing,' the little man mumbled, pulling his pullovers down, 'funny thing.'

People pushed past with bags of fruit and dogs and birds in cages, but none of them spoke to the man. Then a tall boy came up and stared at the white rabbit for a while.

'How much?' he asked.

'Twelve and sixpence,' the last man said. 'It's Dutch.'

24

'Half a bar,' the boy replied.

'Done,' said the last man and handed over the rabbit.

The tall boy left, talking into the rabbit's ear. The last man pulled at the string on the unicorn as Joe came up to pat its head. The unicorn licked Joe's hand.

'He's a bit twisted,' the man said to Joe, 'but he'll grow straight in time.'

'He is a bit twisted,' Joe replied, looking at the unicorn's hind legs, 'and one leg is shorter than the other at the back.'

'He's a runt all right,' the man said. 'Still.'

'How much is he?' Joe asked.

'Only five shillings,' the man said.

'Give you two shillings,' Joe said.

'Come orf it,' the man said.

'He's a bit twisted,' Joe said.

'What if he is a bit twisted?' the man replied. 'He'll grow.'

'Give you two and fourpence,' Joe said.

'Kids,' the man said, 'kids.' He turned into the arches, the unicorn limping beside him, and Joe behind them both.

Under the arches the air smelt of smoke and horses, and footsteps and voices echoed through the smell. In the corners old men with long beards and old women with feathers stuck in their hats, all wrapped up in rags, sat on sacks talking to themselves. As Joe passed, an old man took a long draught from a bottle, and coughed. At the other end of the arches the last man began to hurry, and the unicorn tripped and skipped after him.

When Joe caught up with him the man stopped and the unicorn sat down.

'You still 'ere?' the man asked. 'Kids.'

'What will you do with him?' Joe said.

'Have him for dinner,' the man said.

'Oh,' Joe gasped.

'With a few onions,' the man said.

'How much is he?' Joe asked.

'How many more times?' the man said. 'Five shillings. He cost me that to raise.'

'If you come back with me to Mr Kandinsky at Fashion Street,' Joe said, 'he'll give you five shillings.'

'All that way?'

'And I'll give you two and fourpence as well,' Joe added.

'Give me the two and fourpence, then,' the man said, and Joe counted the coins into his hand.

'I don't mind leading him,' Joe said, 'if you're a bit tired.'

Back at the workshop Mr Kandinsky was fixing the zip fastener into the trousers because, after all, the customer is always right, even when he's wrong. He was talking to the baker from the corner. 'You know,' he was saying, as Joe came in leading the unicorn, 'the black bread agrees with me better, only I get the heartburn something terrible.'

'I'm telling you,' the baker said, 'it's the black bread. I'm a baker, shouldn't I know?'

'Hello, Joe,' Mr Kandinsky said, 'what you got there?'

'Cripple, ain't it?' said the baker.

'It'll grow,' the man said.

'Can you lend me five shillings to pay for this unicorn, Mr Kandinsky?' Joe said.

'For a unicorn,' said Mr Kandinsky, reaching for the box he kept his change in, 'five shillings is *tukke* cheap.'

Later, Mr Kandinsky made a careful examination.

'Clearly,' he said, 'this unicorn is without doubt a unicorn, Joe; unmistakably it is a genuine unicorn, Shmule. It has only one small horn budding on its head.'

'Let's see,' said Shmule. Then after he looked and felt the horn bud he said, 'Granted, only one horn.'

'Second and still important,' continued Mr Kandinsky, 'Joe went to the market to buy a unicorn. That is so, Joe?'

Joe nodded.

'Consequently,' Mr Kandinsky continued excitedly, 'it follows that he wouldn't buy something that wasn't a unicorn. In which case, he bought a unicorn, which is what this is.'

'There's a lot in what you say,' replied Shmule, 'although it looks like a baby goat; a little bit crippled, that's all - not like a horse, which is, after all, a unicorn except for the horn.'

'And this has a horn, yes or no?' asked Mr Kandinsky.

'Definitely,' replied Shmule, 'it has an undeveloped horn.'

'One horn only?' asked Mr Kandinsky.

'One horn,' agreed Shmule.

'So,' concluded Mr Kandinsky, 'it's not a unicorn?'

'What do I know?' said Shmule, shrugging his shoulders. The shrug reminded him of his shoulder-muscles, so he went on flexing and unflexing them for a while.

Then Mr Kandinsky sent Joe to the greengrocery to buy a cabbage and some carrots. 'And a couple of heads of lettuce as well,' he added. 'What he don't eat, we can put in the stew.'

While Joe was gone, Mr Kandinsky examined the unicorn again, while Shmule practised a half-Nelson on himself.

As he ran his hand over the unicorn, Mr Kandinsky sang:

'One kid, one kid, which my father bought for two farthings.'

CHAPTER TWO

Shmule looked around. 'That's what I say,' he said. 'A kid.'

'What harm will it do, Shmule,' asked Mr Kandinsky, 'if we make it a unicorn? Oy,' he added, 'he really is crippled.' Sadly beating his fist on the bench Mr Kandinsky sang:

'Then came the Holy One, blessed be He,
The angel of death to destroy utterly
That struck down the butcher
That slew the ox
That drank the water
That quenched the fire
That burnt the stick
That beat the dog
That bit the cat
That ate the kid.'

Shmule's low voice joined Mr Kandinsky's cracked one in the chorus. Together they finished the song.

'One kid, one kid, which my father bought for two
farthings.'

A LL the excitement about the unicorn was one thing, but Shmule had his own troubles. Second, there was the dreaded Python Macklin, but first there was Sonia.

Sonia was the daughter of Hoffman the butcher, and maybe plenty of meat was the reason why she was the strongest girl between Bow Church and the Aldgate Pump. She was four inches taller than Shmule, and she had only three muscles less than him, and those muscles anyway it didn't suit a girl to have. She could lift Shmule as easily as he could lift Joe, and though she had squinty eyes and a bad temper, she had a very good figure. One day, Mrs Levenson, the corsetière, who did a bit of match-making on the side, got him over to Hoffman's for Friday night supper, and in no time Shmule found himself engaged to Hoffman's daughter Sonia. That was his number one trouble, for although a promise is all very well in its way, what is the use of being engaged if you haven't got a ring to prove it? And Sonia hadn't a ring.

That ring. Sonia didn't forget it for a minute. In the evenings or at week-ends when they practised weight-lifting together and catch-as-catch-can, she never forgot. Shmule might say, 'I pulled a muscle' - that's all. Just 'I pulled a muscle.'

'You got a muscle?' Sonia would ask, insinuating.

'Don't worry about me,' Shmule would tell her, 'I got enough muscles.'

'I forget,' Sonia would answer, lifting up the heavy bar; 'it's diamonds you are a bit short of just now.' Always on for a ring.

Do Sonia justice, the other girls in the blouse factory where she worked wouldn't let her forget. Every day one or other of them tried to needle her about the ring. 'Funny thing,' Dora the blonde - blonde ! - said, 'funny thing a fellow proposes but no ring. You sure, Sonia, he said *marry*?' And even worse. Sometimes girls ran up and down showing off the rings their fellows had given them, and then Sonia felt so small. But she couldn't tell Shmule all that. The only thing to do was to keep at him, because, give credit, a girl engaged is after all entitled to a ring. Say what you like, right is right.

Because of that ring Shmule went in for the wrestling. Before that, he took three pound seventeen he saved in a slate club the baker ran, and bought a gold ring with a little tiny diamond in it. Shmule went into fourteen shops until he found a ring for that money, because everyone knows nothing but diamonds is right for engagements. But he could have saved himself the trouble. He went round to Sonia that night, pleased as punch, and when they were sitting in the front room just as Sonia was about to start nagging him, he jumped up, ran round the room, and shouted, 'Say no more - you got yourself a ring.' He gave her the ring and held his face forward for a kiss.

Who can satisfy women? A fine kiss that Sonia gave him. With the back of her hand she gave him a slap on the cheek and burst out crying.

'Two years I've waited you should make me respectable with a ring, and what do you give me in the end? A little tiny bit of rubbish, I wouldn't be seen dead in it. Why did I ever say yes to you? Why am I such a fool? Why did I let you take me to Epping Forest that time?' Because that was something else she never let Shmule forget, although there had been no trouble.

To cut a long story short, Shmule explained to Mr Kandinsky, Sonia couldn't wear that ring because such a small diamond after such a long time would make her look ridiculous. The other girls might say, insinuating, 'For such a small ring you must wait two years?' And that was why, answering Mr Kandinsky's question, 'Why be a wrestler?' Shmule took up wrestling. Wrestling he could win enough money to buy Sonia a large ring, and then perhaps she would stop nagging him.

'Why don't you just marry the girl straightaway, and save yourself trouble?' Mr Kandinsky asked. 'Surely this is a practical solution?'

'You think I haven't tried?' said Shmule. 'She won't let me come near her until she gets that ring.'

'Why don't you marry someone who's got a ring already?' asked Joe.

'What can you know about these things?' asked Shmule.

'My mother hasn't got a diamond ring,' Joe said.

'Do me a favour,' Shmule replied, dismissing the whole matter. 'I got enough worries. This dreaded Python Macklin I got to fight soon is no joke.'

But although Shmule had worries of his own, he helped Joe to build a house for the unicorn. They got four orange-boxes and a hammer and some nails, and while Shmule knocked them together he told Joe what he would do if he didn't have to develop his muscles to fight the dreaded Python Macklin. Because wrestling kills you for perfect efficiency, Shmule said. Take Fred Hercules, for instance; no use as a wrestler at all, but still the best developed man in the world. And if you could win a title like Mr World, or Mr Universe, or just plain Mr Europe, you were made. That's what Shmule might have been if he didn't ruin himself becoming a good wrestler. Mr Universe. That was something to be. Mr World. You could sign adverts: I grew my muscles on Brymaweet, signed Shmule; I always use a Rolls-Royce car, signed Shmule. It was a gold-mine, and he had to give it up. 'Turn all that in, my future, Hollywood even, because plenty of Mr Worlds have finished up big stars, just because Hoffman's daughter Sonia must have a bigger ring than any other machinist in Gay-day Blouses.' And Shmule gave one of the orange-boxes such a bang with the hammer the side caved in and they had to repair it before going on.

After the house was finished, while Shmule filled up a few cracks in it with canvas, Joe went back into the workshop.

'So, how is the unicorn's house coming along, Joe?' asked Mr Kandinsky, peering through the steam from pressing, and wrinkling his nose, because after all these years he still didn't like the smell.

'Shmule is worried about that Sonia,' answered Joe. 'She wants him to turn in his future, and not have a Rolls-Royce car.'

'Women,' said Mr Kandinsky. 'But we can't do without 'em.'

'You do,' said Joe.

'I'm old,' replied Mr Kandinsky. 'I have had my share of trouble.'

'Did you want to be Mr World, Mr Kandinsky?' asked Joe.

'Mr Kandinsky is already enough for Mr Kandinsky,' said Mr Kandinsky, pressing hard with his iron and making a great cloud of steam. 'The only thing I could do with, because all this bending over ironing gives me a creak in my back, is a Superheat Patent Steam Presser.' Mr Kandinsky leaned back from the bench. 'You know, Joe, with this patent steam presser all you got to do is open it - so. You put in your trousers - so. Close it - so. Press a handle. Pouf. Up comes the steam. Open. There is your trousers pressed. No smell, no consumption. Not like this: hot up the irons, press a bit, they get cold, wet the cloth, press a bit more, hot up the iron again, breaking your back, your heart, day after day.'

Whenever he thought of it, Mr Kandinsky ran on about the Superheat Steam Presser. Once he took Joe to see one working at a factory in Commercial Road. They watched a boy open and close it while another boy put the trousers in and took them out, and Mr Kandinsky looked sad when they left.

'If a man has to be a trousers-maker,' he said, 'it's a pity he shouldn't have a Superheat Steam

Presser.' On the way home he took Joe into a restaurant and they had sweet lemon tea and biscuits.

Usually when Mr Kandinsky mentioned how he would like a patent presser, Joe spent some time suggesting ways for them to save up for one. But now all he said was, 'Maybe my father will send you one from Africa for your birthday,' because his mind was too busy thinking about the unicorn.

Until the unicorn's own house was finished, he lived in the workshop under a shelf, in a nest made up from odd pieces of material. Joe fed him morning and evening, leaving a bowl of water and milk for him to drink should he feel so inclined. Joe talked to the unicorn between meals so that he shouldn't feel lonely, but though he would make quite a good breakfast, he didn't care much about anything. He just looked at Joe with sad eyes and slowly folded another lettuce leaf into his mouth with a long pink tongue.

'I think,' Joe told Mr Kandinsky, 'that this unicorn is missing his mother and father, but what can you do?'

'What can you do?' agreed Mr Kandinsky.

'But where are they?' asked Joe.

'In Africa, no doubt,' said Mr Kandinsky.

'But how did the baby get here?' asked Joe.

'Who can say? Maybe he was left here when the unicorns left.'

CHAPTER THREE

'But by now he should be grown up,' Joe said after a while.

Mr Kandinsky put down his iron.

'There, Joe,' he said, 'you have a problem. That unicorn should be grown up.'

'But he's not,' Joe said; 'he's no bigger than a dog, not a big dog either.'

Mr Kandinsky thought for a while.

'He is not grown up,' he said at last, 'and you know why? Because unicorns can't grow up on their own. They have to be told how by grown-up unicorns. Same as you have to be told by me, otherwise how will you grow up? Same thing with unicorns, which are, after all, only human.'

He took up his iron again, turned the flat of it towards his face, and spat lightly on it. There was no fizz. 'These blankety irons,' he said. 'What I need is a Superheat Patent Presser.'

That evening when Joe's mother came home from work, she asked first and foremost how the unicorn was. Joe said the house was nearly finished, but the unicorn didn't seem to care, and he told her what Mr Kandinsky said about why the unicorn happened to be there at all.

'Mr Kandinsky knows,' Joe's mother said, 'because he reads so many library books. I've got a surprise for you, Joe.' She brought out a bar of *halva*, a sweet made from honey and nuts wrapped in thick silver paper.

After his supper, Joe ate a piece of *halva*. He broke it into very small bits, arranged them on the table, and ate them one at a time. He was thinking and he thought better this way.

When Joe was in bed his mother kissed him and said goodnight, and was about to leave when he sat up.

'You know,' Joe said, 'Mr Kandinsky wants a Superheat Patent Presser, and Shmule wants to be Mr World, and Sonia, that's Shmule's girl, wants the biggest ring in Gay-day Blouses, and that unicorn wants its mother and father.'

'And what do you want?' Joe's mother asked.

'I'm thinking what,' Joe said. 'What do you want?'

'Whatever you want,' Joe's mother answered. Then she said goodnight again; the whole thing all over again; a cuddle with kisses, a cuddle without kisses, one big kiss, and a few little kisses as she had done since he was young.

THEY called the unicorn Africana, because Mr Kandinsky said that was the name for everything to do with Africa. Straightaway the unicorn began to look a little better. Everybody needs a name, otherwise how can they know who they are? You couldn't call a unicorn Charlie or Hymie, or Kandinsky even, so they called him Africana.

Every morning when he had finished his breakfast, Joe took Africana for a walk up Fashion Street, then across the road and back again past the shirt factory. Africana wore a tartan lead and collar which had belonged to the baker's dog Nicolai, named after the Tsar of Russia, both of whom were dead. The shirt factory was dead, too. It was set back a little from the road, and the whole of the front was covered with torn posters. The big door of the factory was painted a sort of purple which flaked off all the time, and had initials carved on it by the boys in the street. Above the height to which the boys could reach was still part of a large coloured poster which showed a magician in a top hat taking a blue rabbit, two blue pigeons and a large bunch of blue flowers out of another top hat. The roof of the shirt factory had small roofs on it and Mr Kandinsky called it the Kremlin. Beside the door there was a faded board which still said, 'Wanted: Machinists', but no one ever went into the factory and the door had a large iron padlock chained on to it.

The two corners where the pavement curved round to meet the far walls of the factory were sheltered from the wind. In one or other of them there often sat one or other of the old men and women who wandered about the East End wrapped up in rags and carrying sacks, with feathers in their hats and crusts of bread sticking out of their pockets. They only talked to themselves, mumbling all the time, sometimes having arguments alone, and once in a while shouting out so that crumbs of bread flew from their toothless mouths. They were wanderers, wandering through the small back streets, poking into dustbins and hiding empty bottles and rags in their sacks, begging stale loaves from the baker shops, and sleeping under the arches or in the sheltered corners of the shirt factory. No one knew them, or where they came from, or where they went. They had always been there. They were very old.

On Africana's morning walks Joe introduced him to the neighbours. Their first call was the baker, who gave them a coconut biscuit each and remarked on how Africana was growing.

'Do you really think he's growing?' Joe asked, because it seemed to him that Africana was no bigger than before.

'Growing?' said the baker, 'I should say so. And he's walking better into the bargain. Fashion Street agrees with him. You want another biscuit?'

'No, thank you,' Joe replied. But Africana said nothing. He didn't even finish his biscuit.

Whenever it wasn't raining, even in the winter, Mrs Abramowitz, who had a small fancy-button shop, used to sit by the open door on a bentwood chair watching people pass. Joe knew that Mrs Abramowitz meant no harm, but he wished she wouldn't pinch his cheek like a hen's bottom, because it made him feel as if he was going to be cooked, and also it hurt. Whenever she called out, 'So, my Joe, how is your Mummy?' so that Joe would have to stop and talk to her, he tried to keep his cheeks out of her way. But it was difficult to talk to people without turning your cheeks towards them, and Mrs Abramowitz was very cunning. While he was busy and off his guard telling her something, a bony hand suddenly jumped up and two bony fingers caught one of his cheeks. 'What a boychick!' Mrs Abramowitz said, licking her lips as if she was tasting him. She smelt of wintergreen ointment and camphor balls, and wore a cardigan with fancy buttons on it.

Another cheek-pincher was the man with the twisted mouth who had the confectionery and tobacconist. He wore a black Homburg hat all the year round, and tried to cover his twisted mouth by growing a bushy moustache which, although his hair was grey, came out red. But you could still see it was twisted. Everyone got their sweets and tobacco from him, but he was not well-liked, being as he was a fence and an informer, a friend to the police. No one trusted him because he got the street a bad name, although he was very pious and quoted Gems at you when you went to buy a bar of milk chocolate or some Polish fruit bon-bons. His favourite Gem was 'Go to the ant, thou sluggard, consider her ways and be wise,' which he said all the time to his daughter, who also had a twisted mouth, although she couldn't grow a moustache so well to hide it. To Joe he would say, 'There is a time for all things; please don't bring the animal into the shop.' Then when he took the money, 'Two and a half to make you laugh.' Joe never laughed because suddenly, if you got too near, the fingers crawling over the polished counter quick as spiders, jumped up and bit your

and a cannibal king who looked like one of the wanderers. They beat them all. Joe wrestled the cannibal king and caught him in the dreaded scissors grip, so that his back cracked like the chair Shmule broke that time. The cannibal king was stuffed full of bits of stale bread and rags which fell out because he had wanted to steal Africana's horn and sell it. Africana defeated the elephant, and speared one of the tigers, and Joe shot the rest. Then they stopped under a big tree for a picnic dinner, and Africana had some greens while Joe brought his meat and potatoes into the yard to eat. After dinner they went on through the jungle. It was a long trek, but down by the lavatory they suddenly came upon the lost city.

In the distance it looked like the shirt factory, with hundreds of cupolas all made of gold shining in the sun. In the city, which smelt of Keating's Powder, everything shone with big diamonds. Joe put one in his pocket to take back for Shmule to give his girl Sonia. The city was empty, although everything was neat and tidy as if his mother had just cleaned through. In one of the treasure vaults they found a large brand-new Superheat Patent Steam Presser which Joe put on one side for Mr Kandinsky.

Joe and Africana walked down a long road paved with silver cobbles. All the way along were stalls with singing birds and hens and hokey-pokey ice-cream and fritters and jellied eels and Polish bon-bons, and you could take whatever you wanted. At the end of the road there was a huge palace like the Roxy Cinema in Whitechapel Road, shining with coloured lights.

As they walked up to the palace there was suddenly a great thunder of hoofs, and hundreds and hundreds of unicorns came galloping towards them. At the head of them there was an enormous unicorn, his great golden horn studded with diamonds, and beside him a milk-white lady unicorn with a very kind face. Africana shouted out to them, and they ran up to him and licked him all over, because they were his father and mother. On Africana's father's back - and this was the best of all - rode Joe's own father, who lifted Joe up on to his knee.

Then Joe and his father and Africana and his mother and father packed the diamond for Shmule and the Superheat Patent Steam Presser for Mr Kandinsky, and went back through Africa with all the unicorns following them, back, back, all the way back to Fashion Street. That was how Joe brought the unicorns back from Africa where they were lost for all those years.

The afternoon Mr Kandinsky and Shmule went to deliver the rush job it was raining, and Joe and Africana played the game called Africa in the workshop.

Joe was wrestling with a chair which was the cannibal king. He was having a hard time because the cannibal king was becoming a better wrestler all the time because of all the practice. Joe was twisting round into a better position to put the old scissors on him, when he saw a very old torn pair of boots stuffed with rags standing near his head. He looked up. It was one of the wanderers.

The wanderer had an old cloth cap with tickets in it, a big red nose, and a dirty beard all over his face. He held a sack in his hand, and a bottle stuck out of a pocket in one of his two overcoats. His little pink misty eyes peered all round the workshop. He asked Joe, 'Is the old guvner in?' although he could see that he wasn't.

Joe knew at once who it was. He watched him carefully, clenching his fists, but when he walked over to Africana he nearly screamed. It was the cannibal king all right. Joe had no rifle and no pistols and couldn't wrestle and it was real. He stared up from the floor as the cannibal king came closer and closer to Africana.

Then, thank God, Joe heard clattering on the steps and Shmule's voice say he was wet through. He jumped to his feet and ran out of the room. 'Quick, quick,' he shouted, the tears running down his face, 'quick, quick, quick.' They rushed into the room while Joe, biting his lip, followed behind.

The wanderer looked up, squinting his misty eyes at them. 'Ow are ye, guvner?' he said. 'Got any old bits of clorth terday?'

Mr Kandinsky sighed.

'You frightened the boy,' he said. 'Shmule, give him some of the bits and pieces. It's all right, Joe,' he said; 'nothing to worry for, Joe.'

Joe didn't answer. He watched the wanderer fill up his sack. All the time he looked secretly at Africana, with a look like Mrs Abramowitz when she was giving a pinch.

When the wanderer went, Joe saw him stop on the steps. Before turning out into the driving rain he pulled the bottle from his pocket and took a long drink from it. Afterwards, Joe went slowly up the stairs and looked out into the street. The cannibal king was stumbling against the wind, the sack over his back. There was a smell of methylated spirit in the passage-way.

A FTER the cannibal king tried to steal Africana, Joe was more careful. Before putting Africana's collar and lead on for the morning walk, he went out into the street to see if it was safe. Even if it was, he no longer led Africana past the shirt factory, because you couldn't be too careful. He also decided to brush up his wrestling in case it should come to that, so it was good luck that Shmule was just then in a period of intensive training.

Shmule had already beat Louis Dalmatian, who was, to tell the truth, a push-over, and the Stepney Thrasher was off with a broken collarbone. So Shmule's manager, Blackie Isaacs, who ran the gymnasium, thought it was a lucky opportunity for Shmule to do Turk Robert and Bully Bason on the quick, and have a go at the dreaded Python Macklin, who was anyway not in such wonderful shape, he heard, owing to his stomach ulcer proving troublesome because he couldn't leave fried food alone, not to mention the booze. It was Shmule's big chance and Blackie fixed for him to fight Turk Robert and Bully Bason in the same week - Bully on the Monday and the Turk on the Friday.

It wasn't so bad as it sounds, Blackie said, because Bully was being paid off to be disqualified in the fourth for persistent gouging. 'Supposing,' Shmule asked, 'I only lose one eye, do you take half commission?'

'Suddenly,' Blackie said aloud to himself, 'suddenly our Maccabaeus has got the wind up. I'm telling you,' he told Shmule, 'the Bully is being paid off - just keep your eyes closed and scream - it's too much to ask for a five-pound purse?'

As for the Turk, he only had two tricks, a deathly rabbit punch and a back-breaking full-Nelson. 'You're up to that, kid,' Blackie told Shmule. 'I know you won't let us down by letting that deadbeat murder you.' And he gave him a good rub-down.

Though he wouldn't talk to Joe about wrestling, except to say it was a mug's game, Bully and the Turk were on Shmule's mind all the time. Between stitching he weaved his head from side to side, and as he lifted the iron he would suddenly duck. All Joe had to do was watch.

The weather was cold, so by special arrangement with Mr Kandinsky, Africana was sleeping in the workshop, and as the workshop had a double lock for insurance purposes it was safe. Joe could consequently pay more attention to the wrestling business than he could with Africana living in the yard. Someone might get into the yard by climbing over the backs of the houses, but you couldn't break in through a double lock for insurance purposes. Also Africana liked it better in the workshop because it was warm and there was nearly always company. He lay under the bench in the nest of off-cuts, looking with bright eyes from one face to another. He needed rest because he had a bit of a cold.

Mr Kandinsky was worried, which didn't make things easier. He was first of all worried about his rheumatism, which was always worse in a sharp spell. He was also worried about Shmule and all this prize-fighting. He was, into the bargain, worrying about a patent steam presser because with the work short it was getting to be more and more difficult to compete. And now there was the unicorn to worry about as well. 'He don't look so good to me, Joe,' he said. 'A little animal like that should be full of beans, jumping and skipping, not lying about the whole day with hardly appetite for a lettuce leaf unless you beg him to take it.' He bent down to Africana. 'Go on then,' he said, offering a piece of leaf, 'get it down; it'll do you good. Oy - the roimatismus is killing me. And business so bad into the bargain.'

Business was so slow that Shmule said could he spend a couple of afternoons at the gymnasium, especially since he had the two fights coming off and needed all the training he could get; not that he would mind how long he worked if there was the work there, but like this even his finger-muscles would be cramping up waiting for the next pair of trousers; not that he wanted to put the mockers on the business, far from it, but why should he sit here messing about making new patterns when they didn't have the work? 'Do me a favour,' said Mr Kandinsky, 'go and wrestle.'

'Can I come with you?' Joe asked, and Shmule was so pleased to be going off he said Joe could, so long as he didn't talk too much and take his mind off serious matters.

Then, after telling Joe to be quiet, Shmule didn't stop talking all the way to Blackie Isaacs' in Middlesex Street, behind Isaacs' fish shop, which was his real business.

'You see,' Shmule said as they walked round the back streets, 'I got to think of all the angles. Take the Bully, for instance. He may take the duck in the fourth all very well, but suppose he doesn't? Also I got to think of my self-respect. If I can beat him fair, it's better, I don't care what Blackie says. So it's no good you saying don't worry because the Bully is taking a duck.'

'I didn't say don't worry,' said Joe.

'I got to keep after him whether he wants to drop out or not,' Shmule went on. 'After all, that's his business. He can be paid off if he likes; that's not my affair. If it pays him better, good luck to him, let him lose on purpose.'

'Why does it pay the Bully better to lose?' Joe asked.

'You can't tell,' Shmule said. 'Maybe his manager put money for him on me and they got good odds because the Bully is an old-stager and they thought he would wrap me up with no trouble. On the other hand, supposing he don't get thrown out for gouging, and I'm taking it easy thinking, what the hell, no need to break my neck, and the Bully gives me a welt, I'm out. No, say what you like, no matter what, I got a fight on me hands. Then there's the Turk. I see him fight three, four times. True he's only got the two grips, but never mind, you've only got the one neck; he's only got to break it the once, no more. And he's got a nice style the Turk, even if he is a bit past it. He must be turned forty.'

'So old?' Joe asked.

'At least,' Shmule said. 'At that age you haven't got the speed; well, you can't expect it, can you?'

'No,' said Joe.

'But he knows a thing or two all right, all right, one or two tricks to give somebody something to think about and no answer back. I got to keep out of his way and watch out for that little opening, then rush him and give him the lot. Otherwise curtains. Also I'm giving him half a stone, remember, and weight counts in the wrestling. Supposing he gets his knee into me gut, I'm finished, had me lot. Just because he's got the weight. No good complaining then, is it? It's all right for Blackie. He don't have to fight 'em, but if he did he wouldn't be so pleased. Two in a week. I ask you.'

'I ask you,' Joe said, 'I ask you.'

'It's too much, Joe,' Shmule said, shaking his head as they got to Isaacs' fish shop.

'I ask you,' Joe said.

In the shop they were hosing the fish down, being as it was late in the afternoon and still not sold out. Mrs Isaacs, who had a great mane of red hair like a lion and a hoarse whispering voice, sprayed the hose over the floor.

'Hello, Ham,' she said to Shmule, short for Hammer. 'Hello, sonny,' she said to Joe. 'Gonna wrestle him, Ham?' she said, laughing till she coughed.

'Hello, Hammer,' said Miss Isaacs, who was also redheaded, giving Shmule a friendly smile. Sonia made a scene once because she was so friendly, too friendly Sonia said, to anyone in trousers, and Shmule a trousers-maker into the bargain.

''Lo, girls,' Shmule said; 'behaving?' He hitched his shoulders.

'Going to win for me next week, Hammer?' asked Miss Isaacs, with that smile. That was what Sonia called it, that smile. Miss Isaacs looked up from under her long lashes, and her eyes were a nice green-grey, very nice with deep red hair.

'For you alone, Reen,' Shmule said.

'And is Sonia doing well with her weight-lifting then?' asked Miss Isaacs, looking down.

'Such a strong girl,' Mrs Isaacs whispered.

'Very nice,' Shmule said.

'I do admire her,' Miss Isaacs said. 'Sometimes I wish I was a bit more developed myself,' and she gave Shmule that smile again.

'This way, Joe,' Shmule said.

'That Miss Isaacs has got nice eyes,' Joe observed.

'I got no time for such things,' Shmule said.

In the gymnasium, Blackie and Oliver, the second, were putting Phil Jamaica, the coloured boy, through his paces. Blackie smoked a cigar and watched closely, grunting every time Phil Jamaica hit the bag. Oliver was a punchie and you couldn't knock him out, though if he hung one on you, you knew it. He was a porter when there was work, at Spitalfields Fruit Market, and could carry eight baskets on his head at once. He helped out as second and would give anyone a fight for five shillings, hit him all you like. Now he was crouching by the bag, his fists following Phil's. The coloured boy was covered with sweat and his eyes stared fiercely at the bag as if it might hit back if he wasn't careful. Blackie saw Shmule come in and waved his cigar.

'All right, Phil,' he said, 'turn it in.' Oliver sat Phil down, puffing and blowing, and whispered into his ear as he rubbed him down.

'Good boy,' Blackie said, when Shmule told him he was putting in extra training, 'good boy.' Shmule went into the little changing room at the other end of the gym. 'Put 'em up,' Blackie said to Joe, squaring off to him, 'put 'em up and let's see what you're made of.'

Joe got into the proper position of defence and Blackie sized him up, still puffing at his cigar. Then Joe suddenly let go and punched Blackie all over his stomach, so that he swallowed some smoke.

'Turn it in, kid,' choked Blackie, 'I wasn't ready. See the kid?' he said to Oliver; 'a champ in the making. Save it for Phil,' he said to Joe, 'he's in training.'

'What your name, boy?' Phil Jamaica asked Joe. His eyes were not staring now, and he had his breath back.

'Joe,' said Joe.

'Watch that old defence, boy,' Phil Jamaica said; 'you was wide open. You got to watch that old defence or you is cooked. Like this.' He squared up to the punch-bag again, shadow-boxing it like mad.

'Easy, easy, Phil,' said Oliver. 'Easy, easy, boy; don't tax yourself, Phil.' Phil whipped round and shadow-boxed in circles round him. 'Easy, easy, boy,' Oliver said.

'Was you watching the old defence, boy?' Phil asked Joe.

Joe nodded his head.

'Now you show me, boy,' Phil told him.

Joe took up the position of defence again, and jumped into action, weaving round Oliver while Phil Jamaica shouted.

'Box him, boy; box him there, boy.'

Joe was puffed afterwards.

'I watched the old defence,' he said.

'You're all right, kid,' Oliver said. 'Always lead with the right and follow with the left, one-two, one-two, like that. Don't forget, one-two, one-two.'

'One-two, one-two,' said Joe, punching hard.

'And keep up the old defence, boy,' said Phil Jamaica.

'The old defence,' said Joe.

Meanwhile Shmule limbered up. He wore crimson briefs with a white hammer in the corner, and as he lifted the weights his muscles stood up in great bands. Blackie Isaacs watched him, rubbing his hands.

'What a boy!' he said. 'What a boy, Olly! What a boy, Phil! Run a couple of rounds with him, Phil. Take Phil for a couple, Hammer,' he said.

Joe watched them wrestle for a while, but though they threw one another about, and grunted and puffed and shouted, beating the canvas, he couldn't see how it was done. First they walked round one another with their legs bowed and their arms bent. That was all right. Then suddenly one jumped on to the other, but it was usually the one who jumped first who finished up with his back on the floor grunting, while the other one twisted his leg backwards and forwards.

First one, then the other, the black man and the white man, and first a black grunt, deep and dark, then a white grunt, higher and lighter. And Oliver, the second, and Blackie Isaacs shouting first for Phil and then for Shmule, while the two of them twisted round one another on the floor.

While Joe was examining the gym, which was a big shed where they used to smoke fish in the days when it paid, and which still smelt of fish, Shmule won the bout. Joe didn't notice him winning, because he was trying to lift himself up on the horizontal bars, but his arms weren't developed enough. He knew Shmule won because Miss

CHAPTER FIVE

Isaacs was watching from the door, and suddenly
there was a groan from Phil Jamaica, and a quick
beating on the canvas from his hands with palms
which were quite pink, and Miss Isaacs shouted
out, 'Great, Hammer.'

Afterwards they had fish and chips in the frying tonight part of the shop, Blackie heaping
their plates with great mountains of golden chips
and fillets of plaice, all very good because the
establishment used only the best frying oil.

While they ate, Blackie talked to Shmule about
his two coming fights and what he had heard
about how both the Bully and the Turk were
finished.

'Get your scissors well up,' Blackie told him.

'And watch the old defence,' Joe told him.
'Lead with the right, one-two, one-two.'

As Joe took up the position of defence two
chips dropped off his plate, one-two, on to
Mrs Isaacs' clean floor.

NO one expected Shmule to lose his two fights, but at the same time, to win two fights in the one week is very good and you shouldn't expect it. Consequently when Bully Bason was disqualified in the fourth round, due to persistent gouging, and Shmule went the whole length with Turk Robert to win on points after a hard fight and fairly clean, everyone was delighted.

People kept dropping into the workshop to congratulate Shmule and ask him how it felt to be a champ in the making, and what he thought his chances were against the dreaded Python, and how their money was on him. It was just as well work was a bit short, otherwise it would have been held up, and that means dissatisfied customers, which is very bad for business. So that if business is bad anyway and held up, at least you aren't losing goodwill.

'Nevertheless,' said Mr Kandinsky, 'with the best goodwill in the world, a patent presser can still be a help, because in the long run people want good work, but they want it cheap as well; and how can handwork be so cheap?'

Business all over the East End was, as a matter of fact, a bit slow, and Joe's mother got a couple of days off. Not that it was a holiday. She was piece-working at the milliner's and consequently didn't get paid if there was no work. But Madame Rita, her boss, a big fat man with very fine fingers, swore that it was often like that just before the spring started, and the weather was after all extra cold for the time of the year. Without sunshine to wear them in, who wanted hats? All the rain and sleet would ruin a good hat, and in bad weather who anyway would be bothered to notice whether a customer wore a new hat or not?

Joe's mother had plenty to do at home. She ran herself up a dress on Mr Kandinsky's machine, a green dress with a small red flower in it, and she made Joe three shirts and a linen jacket for the summer, if it ever came. The net result of all this being that Joe was at a loose end, because women don't talk much when they are making things, and there were so many people in and out of the workshop to talk to Shmule and Mr Kandinsky about the wrestling, that he couldn't get a word in. As for Africana, except for his bit of a sniffle, which was only seasonable since most people were coughing and hawking and sniffing and sneezing, he was all right, although he still didn't want to play about much. Joe could play the Africa game silently, but it wasn't so real indoors, especially if you had to be quiet, and you did have to with so many people about.

Though Joe kept a careful look-out, there was no sign of the cannibal king. His spies must have told him that Joe was learning a trick or two, and knowing what was good for him, he kept away from Fashion Street. But you could never tell when he might strike, so Joe mounted guard three times a day at the doorway, well muffled up against the cold weather for the time of the year.

As it turned out it was just as well, because on the Tuesday he was sucking a bon-bon and thinking that he might as well go down and at least listen to other people talking, when he saw the cannibal king turn into the street.

Joe pressed himself against the wall of the passage and waited. Sure enough the cannibal king stopped when he got to the workshop, bending down to look into the window below the grating. He watched quietly for a moment. Then he stood up, took his nose between his fingers and blew it. Then he took a piece of paper out of his pocket and studied it for a while. Afterwards he folded the paper up carefully, took a last look through the grating, and walked on.

Joe watched him the whole time. That piece of paper was his plan for stealing Africana, and the only thing to do was to follow him, find his lair, and tell the sweetshop man, the informer, who would then tell the police. As it was only cold and not raining, Joe waited until the cannibal king was a bit ahead, and followed.

All the way along, Joe watched the cannibal king carefully, ready to take up the position of defence at a moment's notice. But the old man didn't look back once, which showed how cunning he was, trying to make Joe think that he didn't know he was being followed.

Once he sat down on the kerb for a short rest, and Joe turned to look into the window of a magazine shop where there were thousands of covers in full colour. They showed horrible monsters about to eat beautiful ladies with torn dresses, and rockets going to Mars, the red planet of mystery, and boxers beating one another bloody, and cowboys shooting and gangsters shooting and Huns shooting. Joe was thinking that the pictures were exciting but not very real because you never saw things like that in Fashion Street. He started to think then how it would be if when he got back to Fashion Street a whole lot of horrible monsters were trying to get into the greengrocer's shop to eat Mavis, and her overalls were torn. When he looked round, the cannibal king was gone, which again went to show how cunning he was.

There was a little sunshine now, not much warmth in it, but it made things look brighter, especially the small pools of ice in the gutters. After looking round for the cannibal king for a while, Joe began to carefully break the ice with his heel.

Joe had just found a small pool which was solid ice safe for skating on with the toe of one foot, when there was a great clanging of bells. A fire engine rushed past, covered with ladders, hoses and firemen in helmets, the brass everywhere gleaming in the cold sunlight, the engine bright red and glossy as it flashed past. In case the fire was nearby, Joe ran off in the direction the fire engine had taken.

Joe ran a long way keeping a sharp look-out for fires everywhere, but it was no good. The fire engine had disappeared. It's always the way with fires. You never see them, because they're tucked away somewhere you never dream could catch fire, like the one just round the corner that time when some curtains caught alight. Joe heard the bells and ran all over the place, but when he finally went round the corner, there was the engine with all the firemen standing about, and a lot of people watching, but of course the fire was out.

Joe sighed. He could tell from the way his stomach felt that it was dinner time, and since the old cannibal was nowhere to be seen, he might just as well go home. He would have gone straight home, except that he noticed the big chocolate advert over the railway bridge, and being so near, thought he might as well have a look at Itchy Park to see if any flowers were coming up yet.

Itchy Park was an old graveyard which, though full up, had hedges and a few big old trees. Flowers grew up round the graves, which were so covered with grass that without the gravestones and monuments you would think it was a real park. There were two iron benches painted dark green for your convenience, should you happen to be tired, and in nice weather old men used to meet there to talk politics, while mothers pushed their babies in prams, and children played Release round the graves. With its white stone pillars with iron fences between them, the iron all black and green, the stone all white and black and grey patches from the rain and smoke, it was like ancient Greece. In nice weather, a pleasant place for a short outing.

At Itchy Park the sun made the white stone pillars and whitened headstones shine like alabaster, and Joe dawdled between the graves on his way to one which, last spring, was covered with crocuses. He spelt out some of the shorter words which could still be read on the stones, because even if he didn't go to school yet, Mr Kandinsky told him, there was no need for him to be ignorant. He stopped at the memorial with the split angel on it to see if it had split any more lately. It had only one wing and the tip of that was missing, so that if it did split there wouldn't be much of that angel left, and Itchy Park was already short of angels because they got knocked off so easily. Fortunately, the split angel was no worse, so Joe went over to the crocus grave.

Some of the crocuses were shooting and striped dark green leaves showed through the grass which was winter thin and short. One of the crocuses was quite large but it looked as if it would never flower and felt stone cold. In spite of the sun, blasts of wind cut through the graveyard like wet stone knives. It was no wonder if the flowers were frozen stiff, and the grass thin, and the angels splitting. Standing up to breathe on his fingers, Joe saw the cannibal king.

Why he didn't see him straight away Joe couldn't imagine, because he was sitting on one of the iron benches with his sack beside him, drinking from his bottle. If Itchy Park was his lair, it was certainly a cold one, although maybe one of the graves opened secretly and the king crept into it at night. Joe knelt down again behind the headstone on the crocus grave to watch.

Between taking long drags on the bottle, the king grunted and coughed, not a short dry cough like a dog, but a large wide wet rackety cough, as if his whole chest and stomach coughed with him. The choker round his throat opened and his neck showed loose skin red and raw. There was spit all round his mouth, and his eyes ran with water. As he drank and coughed he only looked like an old man in a graveyard with a bad cold in the cold time of the year.

Joe was creeping round the back to go home, when suddenly the cannibal king gave an enormous cough which shook his whole body so that his face turned purple. While he was getting his wind back, his face turned white, making his beard look dark and thick. He closed his eyes and sank back on the bench, and the open bottle, which was still in his hand, dipped over so that some of the spirit poured on to his coat.

When he got home, Joe's mother and Mr Kandinsky were full of questions about where he had been and how cold he was. Joe didn't tell them about the old cannibal king. It would have been too difficult to explain why he wasn't a cannibal or a king any more, just because of the cold.

THE morning the spring came, Joe woke up in a circle of sunlight with a breeze blowing softly upon his face. Lying still with his eyes wide open, he listened to his mother's breathing, like the sea in the distance, a ship going to Africa. But because it was the spring, Joe agreed it was only a dream, and jumping out of bed ran downstairs without his slippers on to see if Africana had noticed the welcome visitor.

Africana was indeed awake, and so full of beans, you would never guess he didn't enjoy the best of health. In view of the weather perhaps it wasn't surprising, because with the sun you always feel full of beans and it's a pity to go to bed because you will never sleep. With the sun up in the sky, ripe and heavy like a solid gold watermelon, everyone feels it will be a wonderful day, and sometimes it is.

In the yard, the stones already felt warm. The rotten wood fencing, which oozed in wet weather like a crushed beetle, was dry as if washed up on a beach somewhere, near pirate treasure. A weed had grown in a minute of the night on the small patch of bare ground, which in the sunshine was earth not dirt any more. It might grow into a palm tree.

Africana, awake in his house, scratched at the walls, eager to play. When Joe lifted the hook on the door he at once ran out. There wasn't time for a complete game, however, because Mr Kandinsky came into the yard in his carpet slippers and quilted dressing-gown, blinking, his eyes still creased up from sleeping. He sent Joe up at once to get dressed, and put Africana back in his house until after breakfast at least. As he ran upstairs Joe felt his own face just below the eyes, but there were no creases. He guessed Mr Kandinsky had more skin to work with.

Joe's mother's boss, Madame Rita, was quite right: there was more work going in the millinery once the worst of the winter was over. Before the spring arrived, women, like the crocuses in Itchy Park, felt it near, and began to peep round at hats. They were already, during the short spells of sunshine, looking into the window of Madame Rita's shop and saying that it wouldn't really suit me, Sadie, it's for a younger woman, and Sadie was saying but it would, Ada, it's just your style. The next stage was, they came into Madame Rita's and tried on the hats. They tried twenty hats with the brims up, then down, then sideways, then without the trimming, then with more trimming. Madame Rita watched them, his hands on his large belly, a soft smile on his face, a small black cheroot between his teeth. As they tried one hat after another, with or without trimming, he made little soft cooing noises. 'Pardon me, lady,' he would say eventually, 'the brim up is more your style.' With a push here and a push there he made the hats suit the faces they had to sit over. In the end the ladies sometimes bought the hats.

Consequent upon there being more work in the millinery, Joe's mother was kept busier and busier at Madame Rita's, putting on more and more trimming as fashion demanded, and though this is tiring, it is just what the doctor ordered for piece-workers. But they have in consequence to hurry over breakfast. The day spring came, Joe and his mother had boiled eggs, and before she had her coat on, Joe kissed her good morning and ran down to the yard - so you can tell how he hurried if his mother hadn't even left yet, and she in such a hurry as well.

The reason why Joe was in such a hurry that morning was that in his sleep he had thought of a new game and wanted to see if it would work.

One of the things about games is that unless you keep adding to them and working out new ideas, they get dull - not the games really, but you get dull in the games, and then they seem dull. And games like the game called Africa are worth keeping fresh, you must admit, so no wonder Joe didn't bother about such things as turning his egg-shell over and smashing the other side of it. Sometimes there are more important things to do in life than just playing about with egg-shells, and things like that have to give way to Africa. Anyhow, you can smash egg-shells anytime, but you don't get a new idea every night you sleep.

When Joe's mother was leaving, she looked in to Mr Kandinsky's workshop to say good morning to him and tell him that she might be late, and not to worry. Mr Kandinsky pointed to the back window and nodded. Looking out, Joe's mother saw Joe talking to Africana, and waving to someone a long way off. She thought how the back of his neck was still like a baby, delicate, with a little gentle valley down the centre, because he was, after all, almost a baby with everything yet to come. How much they had to learn, what a terrible lot they had to learn. She ran away to Madame Rita's to trim spring hats for those who had already learned what suited them.

All that morning Joe and Africana played together in the yard, which, due to the dry rotten fencing, had become a ship, with old wooden walls. Joe was the captain and Africana on one occasion mutinied. He ran to the other end of the yard frightened by Joe shouting out, 'Fasten your jibs and loosen your mainsails, you lousy lubbers,' which is only what captains do say. That nearly spoilt the game, but they went on, after a pause for Africana to eat a cabbage leaf. They visited the South Sea Islands, where Joe drank coconut milk, which is quite like ordinary milk. Mr Kandinsky brought it out for him in an enamel mug. They found pirate treasure just under the lavatory door, a small black pebble which, when properly cut and polished, would be a black diamond. Then at last they came to Africa and had a few adventures there, but suddenly Joe felt like a talk with Mr Kandinsky. Africana's sniffle had started again so they hurried on to the lost city, met Africana's parents and Joe's father, and came home quickly. By air, as a matter of fact, the unicorns growing large wings like geese for the purpose.

The reason why Joe felt like a talk was that though it was a nice thing to have a unicorn, Africana often didn't seem very interested in playing. Sometimes he sat down in the middle of a game and just chewed, which was certainly irritating, even if he did have a cold. Joe was worried too because Africana still wasn't growing much and his horn was so tiny it couldn't even grant small wishes yet. Joe once wished on it for his mother to come home at three o'clock and take him to the pictures, and instead she came home at turned six and cried because there was no letter from his father.

Whilst locking Africana up, Joe practised talking and spitting at the same time. It was a question of holding the spit loose round the tip of your tongue, which you kept between your teeth, and blowing when you spoke. With a little more time, Joe would have it perfect; but where did they get those sandwich boards from? Joe went into the workshop.

'Where do they get those sandwich boards from, Mr Kandinsky?' he asked.

'Where?' answered Mr Kandinsky. 'A question.'

'From the kingdom of heaven?' suggested Joe.

'Only the religious ones,' Mr Kandinsky said.

'From the agency near the arches,' Shmule said, without looking up from a turn-up he was turning up. 'I know, because Blackie Isaacs has got six of them going round with me on them versus the dreaded Python Macklin at the Baths next Saturday night. No wonder I'm worried.'

'Shmule,' Mr Kandinsky cried, 'you never said nothing.'

'Can anyone get sandwich boards near by the arches?' asked Joe.

'You fighting the dreaded Python so soon?' Mr Kandinsky went on. 'How come you are fighting him? Him next to the champion and you a new boy in wrestling almost.'

'Look,' Shmule said, 'Python is warming up, see. He's near the crown five, six year. Already he fights the champ five times. Four times he loses, once he draws. Now he wants plenty of fights, get into form and knock off the champ, who is boozing too much anyway, quick. Afterwards, plenty exhibition bouts with big money for a couple year, and buy a pub in Wapping. So with the shortage in class wrestlers, Blackie does me a favour. Also knocking off the Turk and Bully didn't help me. I'm a gonner.'

'It's wonderful,' Mr Kandinsky said, 'to think in my workshop a future champion. Wonderful.'

'Wonderful,' Shmule replied. 'I got trouble, so by you it's wonderful. I'm a gonner, I tell you.'

'What kind of spirit is this?' Mr Kandinsky asked sternly. 'A nice carry on. I'm ashamed.'

'You're ashamed. You should have the worry and you wouldn't have no time to be ashamed.' Shmule threw his needle and thread down. 'That bloody Python is going to break my bloody neck.'

'Think how proud Sonia will be of you,' Mr Kandinsky said.

'Sod Sonia; let her fight the Python and I'll be proud,' answered Shmule, and he picked up his needle and got on with his sewing.

'The sandwich boards, Joe,' said Mr Kandinsky. 'The sandwich boards is an interesting case.'

'Sod the sandwich boards,' said Joe. 'That bloody Python.'

'Go to the corner and get three rolls,' shouted Mr Kandinsky in a voice of thunder, and Joe ran out. 'A fine attitude to life,' Mr Kandinsky told Shmule, his mouth turned down at the corners, which was always a bad sign.

When Joe came back he found that Shmule and Mr Kandinsky were not on speaking terms, except for essentials like 'Pass the black thread' and 'Give me the shears.' Joe couldn't break the ice by talking about what was on his mind before he thought of the sandwich boards, because he couldn't remember what it was, so after dinner he went out and spent the afternoon helping Mavis in the shop. At least Mavis always thought it was a wonderful day. She let him serve Mrs Abramowitz with a pound of Granny Smith apples, of which she was very fond. Of course Mrs Abramowitz managed to pinch his cheek, sod her.

THE day before Shmule's fight with Python
Macklin, the workshop was closed. Shmule
was getting into top shape down at Isaacs'
Gymnasium and Blackie was giving every assis-
tance, including sending out of his own pocket a
case of bad whisky to Python, because even if it
would be hell for the stomach ulcers, who can resist
the gift of an unknown admirer? Mr Kandinsky
did have, to tell the truth, a couple of things he
could have got on with, but instead he spent the
morning at Shafchick's vapour bath. By permission
of Madame Rita, Joe spent the morning down at
the milliner's with his mother, which certainly
made a change from all the bad temper and arguments in Kandinsky's workshop. Furthermore, the
girls at Madame Rita's gave you sweets all the
time, and had a completely different kind of
conversation.

Joe's mother was the trimmer, and there was another girl called Sophie who was learning the trimming from her. There was the machinist, Mrs Kramm, who was old and had a chest, and a pretty assistant from the shop named Ruby but called Lady R. Ruby was very nice to Joe, but she treated the others, even Joe's mother, a bit haughty. As soon as she went out of the workroom they talked about her.

'What a fine lady, I don't think,' said Sophie.

'Some lady, I should say, and what was she before? - a little snot-nose giving the boys eyes the whole time,' wheezed Mrs Kramm.

'She's very pretty,' Joe's mother said, picking up a small bunch of artificial cherries. 'And good at her job.'

'That you can say again,' Mrs Kramm said. 'That job she can do all right, I wouldn't wish it on my worst enemy, such a job as she can do so well.' She pressed the treadle of her machine so that the thread shot through the needle like lightning.

'Mrs Kramm,' Joe's mother said, looking towards Joe, 'I'm surprised at you. After all, it's only a rumour.'

'Oh no, it's not, Becky,' Sophie said quickly. 'I've seen him after her behind the gown rail carrying on something terrible.'

'Sophie,' Joe's mother said, 'the child.'

'Here you are, Joe,' Sophie said; 'I've found a caramel in silver paper for you.'

'Thank you very much,' said Joe, because they were the soft kind with a nut in the middle, although he would rather have heard some more about Lady R and Madame Rita. But it was just as well Sophie stopped when she did because while he was taking the silver paper off the caramel carefully so as not to tear it, who should come in but Lady R herself.

'Becky dear,' she said to Joe's mother, 'could Joe go an errand? Would you go an errand, Joe sweetie, for Auntie Ruby, dolly?'

'Certainly he could,' Joe's mother said, though Joe didn't as a rule run errands for dollies.

'Will you, dolly?' asked Lady R, bending down and putting her face right close to his. 'For me?'

'All right,' Joe said. Lady R smelt nice at least, and she had large brown eyes and a smooth dark skin and oily black hair very smooth and curled into a bun.

'Bless you, baby,' Lady R said, and suddenly she gave Joe a fat kiss on his cheek, which though better than a pinch is still a nuisance.

The errand was to go round the corner and collect Lady R's genuine French calf handbag which was having its clip repaired. When he was coming back through the shop with the handbag, which was a sack of coal over his shoulder, he saw

Madame Rita and Lady R behind the gown rail, and what Sophie said was true. Back in the workroom his mother got out her handkerchief and licked it and rubbed off Lady R's lipstick, which meant that it had been on his face all the time and he didn't know, which proves you shouldn't go errands for dollies.

'Don't lick me,' Joe said.

'Keep still, Joe,' replied his mother.

'If you lick me clean, you should lick Madame Rita, too, because his face is even worse.'

'Oy,' wheezed Mrs Kramm, 'the cat is in the bag. What goings on. For a respectable woman it's terrible.'

After Joe had been cleaned up he went down into the cellar, where there were a whole lot of old dummies, coloured crepe papers, and boxes. Although he got filthy, it did allow the women to talk about Lady R, which is all women want to do, anyway. For his part he got down to a serious game of Club Row.

He was being an Indian fortune-teller with a green remnant round his head, when he had a happy thought. He thought how the women wanted to talk about Lady R, and how Shmule wanted to win another fight although he had already won two, and how Mr Kandinsky still wanted a patent presser, and how his father hadn't sent for them yet.

So, Joe thought, everybody is always saying
I wish, I wish, and always wanting things. And
straightaway he improved being a fortune-teller
by having Africana with him. Africana wasn't very
much bigger, but his horn was coming along
nicely, just big enough for, say, five or six wishes.

Joe set out four boxes, on which he made draw-
ings with a piece of flat chalk he kept in his pocket
for emergencies. One of his mother in a hat, one
of Mr Kandinsky, one of Shmule and one of everybody else, including Sonia and Mavis. Then he led
Africana, the wish-maker, to each box. After what
was necessary was explained to Africana, he was
very glad to bend his head so that his horn touched
the drawing on each box. And that was how the
wishes were granted. All this took a good deal of
work, so it was not until Sophie came down to the
cellar to call him for dinner that the job was done.

When he went upstairs he still had the green
remnant round his head. Lady R, who was eating
a saltbeef sandwich, waved a pickled cucumber at
him and called him the Sheikh of Araby dolly. If
Joe didn't find something to do in the afternoon
she would spoil everything, because she was that
type. It was good luck that Mr Kandinsky called
in while Joe was eating his second jam sandwich.

As Mr Kandinsky had spent the whole morning at Shafchick's vapour bath in Brick Lane, he
looked very pink and scrubbed, but he wasn't

angry about Moishe, which was unusual. He said to Joe's mother, 'That Moishe, the cap-maker, went too far today. He got cooked.' And he giggled and asked Joe if he would like to come round with him to the Tailors' Union; he had to tell them about how Moishe was cooked.

Moishe, the cap-maker, had a huge belly and was an old friend of Mr Kandinsky. They argued all the time, and always met on a Friday at Shafchick's, where they would argue their way through the hot room, then the hotter room, then the hottest room in the world, and even while they were being rubbed down by Luke, the Litvak masseur, who only used the Russian massage whether you wanted it or not. Luke carefully made up his own bundles of twigs, holding them high in the steam to pick up the heat. He gave you a rub-down like an earthquake, then shook hands and said 'Good health, Reb.' He was a big man with a huge belly, and when he and Moishe stood together you could drive a pair of cart-horses between them. They carried the argument through whilst they drank glasses of lemon tea to put the moisture back into their systems, although they had just gone to all that trouble to get it out.

Mr Kandinsky's arguments with Moishe were mostly political, like Macdonald and Baldwin, which is the best man, or was the Tsar murdered or can you call it execution, or whether the Tailors' Union should run a sick fund or was it placing temptation in the way? In Shafchick's such arguments became heated especially in the hottest room in the world, because at Shafchick's you can always rely on the heat. They say that Shafchick was a great rabbi who was so pious that Barney Barnato wanted to give him something, so being pious he said what else but a vapour bath for the whole East End, and that's what Barney gave him, and of course he became managing director and did very well, so they say, but why not since at Shafchick's you can rely on the heat, day or night. It comes gliding out of a hundred small gratings slowly until the place is like a stew-pot boiling on the gas. No one bothers you, you sit in a deck chair like Bournemouth or the Crimea, play chess, drink your tea, argue, whatever your pastime happens to be. All the time you are getting the benefit of the heat. Rheumatism is melted before it can crystallise round the joints of your bones, veins become less varicose, the lumbago and all creaks in the back are eased, and you get a good rest into the bargain. And afterwards? Don't ask. You feel like an angel walking through the green fields of Brick Lane. If you wanted to, you could fly looking down upon the hills of East London, while everything is fresh about you, as in the morning of life. You smell the *baigels* leaving the bake-oven. Cart-horses make the streets smell like a farm-yard, and the people about you have the faces of old friends. Everything is so good when you come from Shafchick's that once you get the habit you never regret it, even if Moishe's arguments are so ridiculous they make you a bit short-tempered. It is not a real short temper. It is a luxury to make you feel deeper the joy of having lived through yet another vapour-bath.

As they walked over to the Tailors' Union, Mr Kandinsky giggled most of the time, and once or twice he stopped dead, looked down at Joe and laughed out loud.

'How that Moishe was cooked,' he giggled. 'What a hot-pot.'

The Union was in Whitechapel Road, and in the week there were not many tailors there, but on Sunday mornings they filled the room and spread out into the street, chatting in their long coats about this or that, small groups of them for a hundred yards up the Whitechapel Road. Sometimes a master-tailor would come up and say, 'Have you seen Chaim? I got three days' work for him,' and everyone would shout out, 'Where's Chaim? Here's work for him.' The Union room itself was dirty, with dusty windows on which someone had written with a finger, 'Up with,' but they couldn't decide who, so there was no name. The wooden plank floor was smeared with rubbed-out cigarette ends, and the only decoration on the walls was the black-and-red poster which said, 'Wrestling Saturday Night,' with pictures of Shmule and Python Macklin on it. A young coat-maker who happened to be temporarily unemployed was making up a small book at a table below the poster.

At one end of the room there was a trestle table with a big brown enamel teapot stewing on it, a quart bottle of milk, and a plate of rolls and butter. Behind the trestle Mrs Middleton, the caretaker, stood, cutting rolls, pouring tea, and talking Yiddish with some old tailor who, like Mr Kandinsky, looked in to hear what was happening in the world.

At another trestle table, which had benches along both sides, two men were playing dominoes. As Mr Kandinsky and Joe came in, they finished a game, and the bones clicked as four hands smoothed them over for the next, for domino games go on for ever. Two other men drank tea from big chipped enamel mugs they carried in their overcoat pockets.

'So white gold is by you cheap stuff, rubbish?' one said.

'Who says rubbish?' the other replied; 'platinum is better, that's all.'

'Platinum is good enough for you,' said the first; 'you're sure?'

'Another cup tea, Missus,' the other said.

'You didn't pay for the first two yet,' Mrs Middleton answered.

'You short of platinum maybe?' the first said, putting sixpence on the counter.

Mrs Middleton filled the cups up with black tea, and sloshed milk on top. 'Why, Mr Kandinsky,' she said, 'what a surprise.' She always told her friends that Mr Kandinsky was a real gentleman.

'Mrs Middleton, my dear,' Mr Kandinsky said, shaking hands with her; 'what a pleasure to see you. So well you look; ten years younger. How's the boy?'

'He's in the sign-writing now,' Mrs Middleton said proudly.

'A good trade,' one of the men said.

'Very artistic,' said the other.

'You know,' Mr Kandinsky said to the men, 'that boy when he was twelve could draw anything you like: a pound of apples, a couple oranges, a banana - anything.'

'Maybe he should have gone in the fruitery,' one of the men said.

'No,' replied Mr Kandinsky, 'people as well, the King, politicians.'

'Bastards,' the other man said.

'A nice cup of tea, Mr Kandinsky?' asked Mrs Middleton.

'By all means, with pleasure,' replied Mr Kandinsky, 'and a glass of milk for the boy.'

'Your grandson?' asked Mrs Middleton. 'Bless him.'

'Nearly,' Mr Kandinsky said, 'bless him.'

While they drank their tea and Joe sipped his milk, which was a little dusty, Mr Kandinsky asked the men how was business, and they said he meant where was it, it was a thing of the past, tailors were two a penny if you were throwing your money away because in a couple of months the tailors would pay you to let them work. Mr Kandinsky said it was terrible, he was feeling it bad, but what could you do? And the men agreed, what could you do?

All the time Mr Kandinsky was on edge to tell them how Moishe was cooked. He was leading up to it by saying how well he felt after a vapour bath at Shafchick's. One of the men liked vapour baths very much, but the other one thought they were bad for the system, like lemon tea, tasty but rotting to certain organs of the stomach.

'You,' the other man said, 'with a barrel organ in your stomach, you couldn't make more noise, such rubbish you talk. Vapour baths is proven by the best medical authority to be the best thing in the world for the system. Lords and ladies are paying fortunes to go to foreign parts, and why? - because they got vapour baths. And here we got in the East End one of the finest vapour baths in the world, where for practically nothing you can go and sweat first or second class all day long to your heart's content. He isn't satisfied. It's rotting the organs from his stomach, Mr Platinum here.' He spat on the floor.

'Manners,' warned Mrs Middleton.

'Anyhow,' continued Mr Kandinsky, annoyed at the interruption, 'who's telling the story? You know Moishe the cap-maker from Cable Street?'

'The one who married his son to the daughter of Silkin, the wholesale grocer?' one of them asked.

'No, no,' the other said. 'Moishe is the one with the big ears who goes to the dogs.'

One of the men playing dominoes looked up and grunted.

'You know,' he said. 'Everything you know.'

'You know better?' the man replied.

'You know,' the domino player said again.

'So play,' said his partner, who was winning.

'Anyhow,' Mr Kandinsky continued, 'Moishe comes to the baths on Fridays and you think you can argue, but that Moishe is one to argue you out of business. Doesn't matter what you say, he knows better. Whatever it is, politics, history, business, anything, he knows better. I just come from Shafchick's and you know what happened?' Mr Kandinsky stopped to giggle again and to give the domino players a chance to look round from their game. 'He just got cooked.'

Naturally they all wanted to know what happened, so after laughing a bit more to drag it out, Mr Kandinsky told them.

He and Moishe were talking about the slump and he said that if only he had a patent steam presser he could do all right, slump or no slump, because if you could do the work fast enough, it didn't matter if you got paid less, just so long as you kept turning it over, and if you keep working you can always make a living. Also with a patent presser you could take in pressing when the trousers were slack. At once Moishe says what does Kandinsky know about economical matters, leave it to the specialists who get employed to know these things, they take years of study.

'I been studying my trade with the goose-iron for enough years,' Mr Kandinsky replied. 'I know what's what.'

'Kandinsky,' said Moishe, 'that's where you make your mistake. Do you know what is a price spiral with an inflation? You don't. Do you know we are dropping off from the gold standard? You don't. Do you understand the economical problem of today? You should worry.'

'What is all this to do with making trousers for a living, if you don't mind a question?' asked Mr Kandinsky.

'That's what I mean,' replied Moishe; 'trousers-making you know, but what else?'

'And what else am I talking about? I read plenty books in my time and now also, but leave that to one side; what am I talking about except trousers-making? I am saying a patent steam presser is what I need. I don't know what is good for my business?'

But Moishe went on and on about gold prices and unemployment figures. He read the financial column of the paper very carefully every day as a hobby, and he was enjoying himself, especially as there was a shortage of cap-makers and he had plenty of work.

They went into the heavy steam room, where you can hardly breathe or see at all. But in spite of that Moishe went on talking and talking from his end of the room, lying on the marble bench with his towel under him, talking and talking. So Mr Kandinsky left him to it. 'Let him talk to himself, since he's the only one who knows what he's talking about,' Mr Kandinsky thought, as he went out for a massage.

He had his massage talking with Luke the Litvak about his brother-in-law, the doctor in the children's hospital, although, funny thing, no children of his own. After-wards he sat down quietly in a deck-chair in a second-class cubicle. He drank a glass of lemon tea and read the paper. Then he settled down for a little sleep.

Suddenly, just when Mr Kandinsky is dreaming he is picking cherries in an orchard at home, and though the cherries are full and ripe, there is yet blossom on the trees, which is impossible but looks wonderful and the smell, there is a shouting, and he wakes up. There, the colour of borsht and steaming like a pudding, is Moishe, cursing him and saying what a thing to do, locking him in like that, and it's wonderful he's alive to tell Kandinsky what kind of a lousy dog he is.

'And what happens,' laughed Mr Kandinsky, 'is this. I am so fed up with Moishe talking and talking, I slam the door of the heavy steam room, and it jams. I told him, is it my fault the door jams? It's the heavy steam from him talking so much. What's it got to do with me? You should have seen him, just like a stuffed neck he looked, stuffed with red cabbage. Luke and me laughed our heads off.'

The men laughed and said it should teach Moishe to argue the whole time; they must remember to ask him how he got cooked and how was his price spiral. Then they went back to their own arguments, which, since Mr Kandinsky was there, came down to the question who would win the fight tomorrow night. They placed bets with the man who was making the book, and Mr Kandinsky said as it was a special occasion he would put a shilling on for Joe. The platinum man said to the white gold man, 'Even if he don't win,

I don't want to make a crust out of that lousy Python Macklin, who is, without doubt, one of the dirtiest fighters in the ring today. Also if Shmule wins, it's good for the tailors, and we should all be behind him, even if he loses.'

Joe put down the buttered roll he was eating.

'Shmule will be the winner,' he said.

They all looked at him in silence for a moment.

'Put another bob on, Hymie,' said white gold.

'Out of the mouths of babes,' said Mr Kandinsky.

Just at that moment one of the old men stopped clicking dominoes and said to Mr Kandinsky, 'Kandinsky, you want a patent presser? My brother-in-law, the one with the big factory.'

'Big factory,' the other old man said.

'You got a bigger factory?' the first old man asked.

'So?' asked Mr Kandinsky.

'He just got a new presser for his new factory, and he's chucking out the old one.'

'It works?' asked Mr Kandinsky.

'To look costs nothing,' the old man said.

'So I'll look,' replied Mr Kandinsky, and patted Joe's head.

Joe was very pleased, especially when you remember that Africana wasn't really with him in the cellar at Madame Rita's. It may have been the green remnant, because you can never tell where an odd bit of magic is going to turn up, so why not in the cellar of Madame Rita's? Joe thought they had better get home quickly now, because it might start to happen any minute.

The first thing Joe did when they got home was to go into the yard and thank Africana. He put his arm round his neck and kissed him gently on the head, next to his horn bud. Africana coughed and his head jerked up and hit Joe's jaw, making him bite his tongue.

THE following day the weather was cold again. It was going to be one of those springs which stops and starts, unable to make up its mind whether to stay or not. One moment the stone streets were pink and bright in the sunshine, and the next they were grey and dirty again, the sun sunk away somewhere behind a million chimneys on a million slate roofs. But though Saturday morning brought no quick pools of sunlight and the Kremlin, a disused shirt factory, looked blank and dead in the grey light, no one bothered, for they were all impatient for the evening. Once the evening comes, what does it matter how bright or dull the day has been? So far as the evening is concerned, all days are bright, and tomorrow can be still brighter. Hurry along tomorrow, a brighter day, and for an overture, let the evening bring great moments of life such as the spectacular fight between the Aldgate Hammer and the dreaded Python Macklin. And for the sake of tailors everywhere, let the tailor win.

Shmule gave Mr Kandinsky four seats in the second row for Joe and his mother, Sonia and himself. The fights didn't begin until half-past seven, and Shmule's bout came up an hour later. Mr Kandinsky was going to get them there in good time for Shmule's fight, but he would in no circumstances hear of them seeing the fights which came before.

'We are not,' said Mr Kandinsky, 'savages to go and watch the gladiators fight and to enjoy the struggles of people we don't know. Shmule is our own boy, so we must encourage him, not have a good time while other people get broken necks. If it wasn't for Shmule fighting we would never go, not in a hundred years.' And even Sonia, who enjoyed wrestling even if she didn't know the wrestlers – and she knew most of them, of course – had to wait round the house talking about her trousseau with Joe's mother until it was time to leave.

Africana was shivering. Joe tried to make him comfortable in his house, which had had so many bits and pieces tacked on to it through the winter that it looked like a wooden patchwork quilt. It was a shame that animals weren't allowed at the wrestling, because if Shmule did win it would be Africana's doing. Joe promised to tell Africana everything in the morning, and anyhow Africana's cough was bad. He wouldn't take Gee's Linctus, even on cubes of sugar, and what with the break in the weather making it treacherous for bronchial complaints, it was just as well for Africana to stay at home. Joe told everybody that Africana wasn't very well. Being the first dressed, he went out to have a word with Mavis on the subject.

The street looked quite different at night. Great deeps of shadow gathered in the corners of the Kremlin, and the small shops were warm with lamps. The baker's lamp was gas and spluttered, but Mavis's were electric and steady. On the street corner there was a barrow with a big naphtha lamp spitting away white and blue, and two large iron braziers with iron trays red hot on them, roasting chestnuts and baking potatoes. Someone stood by the barrow, and Joe was surprised to find it was the man who helped the Eel King on Sundays, so it looked as if with the coming of the night everyone became someone else. Even Mavis looked different, older and paler in the yellow light, with tired markings on her face, her flowered overalls dirty from where she had clasped bins of potatoes all day long. She was surprised to see Joe up and about at that time of night.

'You do look a toff, Joe,' she said, 'in long trousers and a jacket to match, a real toff. Where are you off to? You should be in bed.'

'Yes, they are nice,' Joe said, putting his hands deep into the pockets of his long trousers. 'They have real flies, with buttons.'

'I suppose old Mr Kandinsky run them up for you,' Mavis said. 'He run up all my old dad's.'

'You look a bit old, Mavis,' Joe said. 'The whole street looks sort of different at night.'

'I am a bit old, dear, I reckon,' said Mavis, 'and with the end of the day you feel it more.'

'You'll have to hurry, because we're going soon,' Joe said, and told her about Shmule's fight.

'I shan't come, Joe dear,' Mavis said; 'there's still a lot to do, though no morning market to think about, and I don't think blood sports should be allowed anyway, and wrestling is a sort of blood sport. Would you like a nice apple?'

'Thank you,' said Joe, taking a large bite of the russet apple she handed him. 'What's a blood sport?'

'Where they hunt poor dumb animals,' Mavis said, 'for their sport, like the early Christian martyrs and saints that were thrown to the lions.'

'You mean the lions ate them up?' Joe asked, thinking it was a good thing he never did get that lion cub for a pet.

'Yes, poor souls, limb from limb,' said Mavis, sorting through the tomatoes.

'They must have been hungry,' Joe said, taking another large bite of his apple.

'It wasn't them, poor dumb beasts, it was the sinfulness of their masters; and yet, Joe, they prayed for their torturers in the midst of their torment.'

'What's torturers and torment?' Joe asked, although he really wanted to talk about Africana.

'Don't trouble your head about it,' Mavis said. 'Oh, what a rotten one,' she added, throwing a soft tomato into a box, where it burst juicily. 'How's your little unicorn?'

'That's what I was going to tell you,' Joe said. 'He's got this bad cold on the chest and coughs all the time, and he's not interested in anything, and won't touch the Gee's Linctus, even on cubes of sugar. Do you think it's the consumption?'

Mavis stopped sorting for a moment.

'He never was very strong, you know, Joe. He was always a delicate little thing. This has been a rotten winter for the best of us.'

'I know,' said Joe. 'Mr Kandinsky has been getting terrible creaks down his back this winter, and I saw someone with a cough.' He was going to tell her about the cannibal king that time in Itchy Park, but he didn't want to think about it.

'Will you have a look at Africana, Mavis?' he said instead.

Mavis closed the shop and they walked down to the house. They went through to the yard, and Mavis wrapped Africana in a piece of blanket and brought him into the workroom. In the light from the naked bulb over Mr Kandinsky's bench Africana looked pinched and sick, and Mavis's face was serious. While she examined Africana, Joe heard Mr Kandinsky call from the other room and went to see him.

Mr Kandinsky was walking about in polished boots, wearing a combination woollen vest and long pants.

'I can't find them blankety trousers,' he said. 'Can you imagine, Joe,' he added, 'a trousers-maker without a pair of trousers to his back? Here they are.' Grunting, he drew a pair of striped black trousers out from beneath the mattress and pulled them on.

Joe told him that Mavis was in the workroom having a look at Africana, who wasn't at all well. Joe made his face serious like Mavis's, the lips pressed tight together.

'That animal,' Mr Kandinsky said, 'has he ever been not sick?'

'Maybe we should send him back to Africa, to his mother and father,' Joe said.

'Africa?' asked Mr Kandinsky. 'What's with Africa?'

'To the other unicorns,' Joe said, a bit annoyed because Mr Kandinsky wasn't thinking.

'Oh my God, yes,' said Mr Kandinsky. 'Africa. Maybe we should. Quite right. Have a wine cherry, but only one.'

Mr Kandinsky's bedroom was almost filled by a big mahogany bed with two large feather beds on it. A huge wardrobe stuffed with clothes and books and remnants took up one wall. The other wall had a small fireplace choked with coloured crepe paper. But in the corner was a small barrel in which Mr Kandinsky made cherry wine. It was the best thing in the room, with a little tap and a mug hanging from it, full of soaked black cherries scooped from the bottom of the barrel, making the room smell always of cherries and wine. Joe took a cherry and put it into his mouth. He tasted the wine while the cherry was still on his lips. Then he bit through to the stone slowly so that the wine-taste spread right through his mouth.

'So,' said Mr Kandinsky, 'I'm ready. Just let me put on my watch. This was my father's own watch and chain, Joe. A real watch, with an albert. So, lead on, Macduff. Forward to the big fight.'

In the workroom, Mavis was rubbing Africana's chest slowly, and talking to him in a whisper.

'Mavis,' said Mr Kandinsky, 'nice to see you. You coming to the fight?'

'This animal isn't at all well, Mr Kandinsky,' said Mavis. She looked in Joe's direction, and moved her head.

'Joe,' said Mr Kandinsky, 'you can take one more cherry yourself and take some upstairs for your mother and Sonia.'

When Joe had left, Mavis said to Mr Kandinsky, 'This poor little soul's torment.'

'Oy,' said Mr Kandinsky.

'It's cruel to leave him,' said Mavis, and she was suddenly very hard and determined. 'It's cruel.'

'What must be, must be,' said Mr Kandinsky. 'But wait till we go.'

'That man should never have sold it to him in the first place. How could it live in Fashion Street?' She stroked the little animal's head just where its stunted horn buds grew so close together as to seem one horn. 'Poor little kid,' she said. 'I'll take it to the People's Dispensary.'

'You're right,' said Mr Kandinsky with a sigh. 'How can a kid like this grow up in Fashion Street? It's not strong enough. I'll find something to tell the boy.'

Joe's mother and Sonia came down the stairs, still talking about Sonia's trousseau. She had a nightdress of pure silk and another one with Flemish lace neck and hem; a shame to wear them really, except in hospital.

Joe said goodnight to Mavis, who held Africana shivering in the blanket. Mavis would look after him, and he was pleased to go into the dark street again. He hurried ahead of Mr Kandinsky and the women, and only for one moment did he want to run back again to Africana.

'*One kid*,' sang Mr Kandinsky quietly, '*which my father bought for two farthings.* Goodnight, Reb Mendel,' he said to Reb Mendel Gramophone, who stood, a little bearded shadow, at the end of the street.

Reb Mendel's gramophone on top of an old pram pushed its big cracked horn towards Joe, and sang in a fast high voice like tin, '*Eli, Eli, lamah azavtani.*'

IN the Whitechapel Road it was all bright lights and crowds of people, smart as paint, taking a Saturday night stroll after working the week as machinists and under-pressers and cabinet-makers.

They queued at the Roxy for the second house, two big pictures, while an acrobat turned somersaults in the road for pennies, and sang *Any old iron*, jangling a string of real medals. They crowded into restaurants for lemon tea, and swelled out of the public-houses waving bottles, their arms about each other's necks, their children waiting at the doors with glasses of lemonade clasped to their narrow chests. They walked slowly along, bright ties and high-heeled patent-leather shoes, eating chips out of newspaper, careful not to let the vinegar spill on to their new clothes. Arm in arm they walked, in trilby hats, brims down, girl-friends with bright lips and dark eyes and loud laughter, mothers and fathers arguing together, calling to children licking toffee apples and taking no notice, old men talking quietly raising their eyebrows, knowing the truth of things.

Joe strode ahead of his mother, who chatted with Mr Kandinsky, while Sonia dawdled talking to a girl with heavy pencilled eyebrows and glossy silk stockings, out with her new fiancé, a bookie's runner and flash with wide padded shoulders to his blue double-breasted suit. Joe took giant strides past Russian Peter with his crooked beard and Russian peaked cap. Russian Peter usually had wreaths of garlic cloves and pyramids of home-pickled cucumbers on his barrow, a large box with handles mounted on two wheels, but now he had a tray with packets of sweets and chewing-gum and toffee apples. Instead of calling out, 'Cumber, knobbel, cumber, knobbel,' as he usually did, he said, 'Taffee eppls, taffee eppls,' in the same high voice. Russian Peter's cucumbers were pickled by a special recipe he brought with him from Russia, with his peaked cap. Joe went back to ask his mother for a toffee apple. Sure enough, it had a special taste, strange, black glistening treacle.

They allowed plenty of time for the walk to the baths, which was just as well, because what with Sonia saying hello to all her friends and their new fiancés, and Mr Kandinsky talking to this one and that, and different people asking Joe's mother how was his father, they would be lucky to get there at all. As it was, when they arrived at the baths, Joe heard a great roar from inside, and thought, that's it, that's the end of the fight; we've missed it. But they hadn't. It was still the last round of the fight before.

For the wrestling season, the swimming-baths were boarded over, a relief to Joe who had been wondering how they could wrestle in baths. There were big lights over a ring in the middle, and you could make out the diving boards at one end, dim in the darkness, with canvas sheets hanging over them. There was no water beneath the boards though, because Joe dropped a small stone through them and there was no splash. It was like the railings over the pavements in the streets. If you made up your mind they were fixed, it was all right. People sat in rows, on seats in front and benches behind, while further back still they stood on wide steps, sitting on the floor in the intervals.

Men went round with trays selling hokey-pokey ice-creams, roasted peanuts, and cold drinks, and there was a great hum of noise, which, during the fights, quietened down so that only one or two voices would be heard over the grunting of the wrestlers. Two wrestlers were tied up together on the floor of the ring, one of them grunting as he pressed down harder and harder, the other shouting out 'Oh, oh, oh, oh!' every time he was pressed. He wore a red mask but he was losing all the same.

Someone called out 'Wheel 'em out,' and someone else shouted 'Carve-up,' and a red-headed woman screamed 'Tear his arms off, Mask.' All around people munched peanuts and drank ice-cold drinks out of bottles. As Joe sat down a man in a big coat started to eat a sandwich and a pickled yellow cucumber at once. At the end of the row where they were sitting, Joe saw Madame Rita and Lady R. Madame Rita had his arm round Lady R. He shouted 'Chuck 'em out, they're empty,' waving a cigar in his other hand. Lady R watched the wrestlers closely. Her eyes stared and her lips moved in a small tight smile, and when one threw the other, she clasped her hands together, breathing out hard between her teeth. Then, when they finished, she sank back in her seat and looked round with shining eyes at Madame Rita, who squeezed her shoulder in case she was frightened.

The end of the fight came while Mr Kandinsky was buying them roasted peanuts. The bell rang, and one of the wrestlers, puffing and blowing, had his arm held up by the referee, while the other one still writhed on the floor. Half the people cheered, and the other half booed. The two wrestlers left the ring, sweating hard, their dressing-gowns draped over their shoulders. One of them tripped on the ropes.

There was a good echo in the baths, although with all the shouting and laughing it was difficult to hear it, but sometimes there was a gap in the noise, people were suddenly quiet, as if getting their wind, and then one voice would ring out and the echo pick the words up and throw them back into the smoke and the smell of ozone. Joe would have liked to shout for the echo, but while it was all right under the arches, you didn't like to in front of so many people, and anyhow as soon as you decided to try it, the noise started again. 'Wheel 'em in,' they shouted. 'Money back, get on with it.' But nothing happened because it was the interval.

At the ends of the aisles St John's men in uniforms with polished peaks and white bands sat looking out for people to faint, but no one did. Programme-sellers went up and down, shouting out that the lucky programme number got two ringsides for next week. Madame Rita had two, but bought two more, just to show off. The hokey-pokey men in white jackets did very well, and almost everyone was sucking orange and pink ice-creams or drinking from bottles or eating peanuts, crunching the shells under their feet.

Then, just as the crowd was getting bored with lucky programmes and hokey-pokey, and restless for the big fight to start, the M.C. climbed into the ring. There was a great roar, and though he held up his arms, it went on. He shook his arms, turning from one side to the other, and the dickie front of his evening suit opened a little. 'Ladees and gentlemen!' he shouted, 'your attention if you please, ladees, your attention gentlemen, please.'

The crowd quietened and the M.C. smiled. 'For your entertainment, at great expense, Sam Spindler, the well-known harmonist, will entertain you.' There was a groan as Sam Spindler, a thin bald-headed man in a Russian silk blouse with red ruching, and black trousers cut wide at the bottom but tight in the waist, climbed through the ropes with a piano accordion, all ivory and silver and red enamel, on his back. He bowed twice and played *Tiger Rag*, getting the tiger so well that lots of people threw pennies into the ring when he finished. Then he played a medley of songs like *My Old Dutch* and *Tipperary* and everyone sang, but when he stopped and got out a piece of wood, took his accordion off and started to tap-dance, the crowd started to boo. He had to play the accordion again, which was a shame, because Joe was interested in tap-dancing and liked to watch the arms and the legs bent at the knees and the little head jerks.

A lot more pennies were thrown, then someone shouted, 'We want Python,' and a whole crowd took it up. Another crowd answered 'We want Hammer,' and soon you couldn't hear Sam playing at all. He stopped and looked down at the M.C.'s seat with a worried expression on his face. The M.C. came up and thanked Sam, who was picking up his pennies. He spread out a big poster on the floor and started to read out the programme for next week, but the noise was so great he gave up. He beckoned towards the dark door through which the other wrestlers had passed after their fight. A little wiry man in shirt sleeves and blue braces came bounding up the aisle, and leaped into the ring. After him marched the wrestlers.

First Shmule, in a crimson dressing-gown gleaming in the light, with Blackie and Oliver bustling round him. A man leaned over to pat his back as he passed, and when he sprang into the ring there was quite a big cheer. Shmule bowed towards the cheers and looked proudly at the small group who booed. He waved to Joe, and Joe waved back. Sonia blew kisses and Mr Kandinsky said, 'A fine boy; good luck to him.' Then Shmule started stretching himself, so as not to lose a moment's development.

After him came the dreaded Python with his manager, a man with a square blue jaw, like polished rock. The Python wore a black silk dressing-gown and a white towel round his neck, and he towered above the seconds dancing round him. He climbed into the ring, not so full of spring as Shmule, but with one powerful hitch of his arm. There was, true, a bigger cheer for Python, but Shmule's friends booed hard, Joe hissed like a goose, Sonia shouted out 'Carcase meat,' and Mr Kandinsky said 'What a bull.'

The M.C. introduced Shmule first. He called him the white hope of Aldgate, the sensational young former amateur championship contender, a clean-fighting local boy, and so on and so forth. All the while the Python was baring his teeth and growling and shaking his fist at Shmule's supporters. Shmule slipped out of his crimson dressing-gown and now his muscles rippled in the ring lights, his spotless white hammer shining like a star against the crimson briefs. Oliver and Blackie clustered round his corner with towels and pails and a chair for him to sit on between rounds. They looked worried, although after all that saying he was a gonner, Shmule looked as if nothing could ever frighten him. There was a fresh feeling about him, as if he felt there were so many tailors expecting him to make a good fight, especially with the trade being so up and down, and so much unemployment, they lent him the strength they had been saving for work.

The dreaded Python Macklin was very angry. He strained like a fierce bulldog at the rope, just waiting for the bell to sound to throw himself on Shmule, tearing him limb from limb like the Christian martyrs, just as Mavis said. The black hair on the Python stood up in fury and he ground his teeth together. When the M.C. pointed in his direction and called out his name, famous contender for the championship of the world, and veteran of the ring all over Europe, the Python drew himself up and the muscles on his chest and back were swollen with pride and power. He grinned, his teeth clamped tight together, and when the red-haired woman screamed out, 'Murder him, Py,' he stared at her as if he was hungry and she was a juicy steak.

'A forty-minute contest,' the M.C. shouted through his megaphone, 'of eight five-minute rounds, for a purse of not ten, not twenty, but twenty-five pounds.'

He drew the two men together and whispered to them, the Python sneering, Shmule looking serious. Mr Kandinsky said again, 'Good luck,' and then the bell rang. In the sudden silence it echoed well.

Joe sat with his seat tipped up to see over the head of the man in front. This man had a head like a smooth water-melon with a bit of hair round the edges, pasted down with oil as if painted. As soon as the bell rang he started to talk slowly in a gruff voice like a gate swinging on rusty hinges in the wind. The woman next to him had grey hair permanently waved and never spoke, except to say, 'Have a nut.' The man was very helpful to Joe because he was an expert and explained the whole fight, hold by hold.

At first the wrestlers circled watchfully round one another looking for an opening. The man with the painted head said, 'You watch, Em; he'll be on to him; just give him that opening; watch, it's coming - no, hold it, now - no, he missed it, he's waiting to put the scissors on him.'

The Python prepared to spring on Shmule, who stood quite still waiting. Then, as the Python bent his legs to jump, Shmule stepped aside and Python fell on his face with a heavy slap.

'He missed him,' said the man with painted hair, and even as he spoke Shmule leapt on to the Python, catching both legs below knee level in the crook of his arm, and pulling sharply.

'Ouch!' shouted Python.

'Ouff!' said the man with painted hair. 'He got the old calf-lock on him.'

The Python shook himself like an alligator, and one of his knees slipped free and bowled Shmule over. The Python caught hold of Shmule by the foot and thigh and prepared to throw him, but Shmule pressed into the canvas with both hands, and heaved his body into the Python's ribs like a battering-ram. The Python reeled into the ropes, and the bell rang.

Shmule turned to his corner, but the Python came after him. The crowd roared with one voice, 'Look behind you!' Shmule turned sharply, and the referee jumped in front of Python, and forced him to his corner. The Python was furious and, pushing his seconds off the ring, he picked up his chair and punched his fist through the seat.

'Phoo,' said the man with painted hair, 'what a round, the dirty bastard turning on him like that after the bell, the dirty great bleeder.'

'Have some nuts, Fred?' the permanently waved woman said.

'The swine,' said Sonia with tears in her eyes; 'did you see that?'

The seconds rubbed them down and waved towels while the wrestlers spat into pails, and breathed deep and even, glaring at one another across the ring, listening to their managers' advice. The crowd wasn't shouting, 'Carve up,' any more. They could see it was serious. The bell rang for the second round.

The Python at once shot from his corner, his fingers crooked to seize Shmule, his face rigid, calling the muscles of his body to attention. Shmule crouched like a panther, waiting.

'He's giving him half a stone,' the man with the painted head said. 'He's got to play a waiting game; let the Python use hisself up, then come in quick. Ahh!'

The Python had his arms about Shmule and was hugging him like a bear. Shmule's arms were pinned to his sides, and he couldn't move. He twisted to one side, then to the other, but the Python short-ened the hug, working the grip of one hand upon the other wrist slowly up his arm. Shmule's face twisted with pain.

'Let him get out of that one,' the man said. Sonia clenched and unclenched her hands, and Joe's mother looked away. Mr Kandinsky was breathing hard, but Joe just stared, wondering what Shmule would do now. The crowd was shouting, 'Finish him, Python!'

Then Shmule moved his hand up and down in fast little movements against his thigh, and the referee, jumping about watching, saw the sign, and told Python to let go, the Hammer gave in. But Python wouldn't let go, and Shmule bit his lips in agony. Now the crowd shouted against the Python, but that didn't help Shmule. The referee and all the seconds jumped on to him to tear him away, and the bell rang.

Blackie and Oliver helped Shmule to his corner and gently rubbed him, putting wet towels on his face. The crowd was furious with the Python, but he didn't care. He shouted back at them, showing off his muscles and asking if any one would like to try them. 'Filth!' Mr Kandinsky shouted, but poor Shmule looked pale and his eyes were closed.

'He's a dirty fighter,' the man with painted hair said, 'but give credit, he's got a grip like iron, the bleeder.'

'Get us some more nuts, Fred,' the woman replied.

Blackie and Oliver were working hard on Shmule, who breathed deeply, the colour coming back into his face. By the time the bell rang for the third round, he seemed as good as new.

'But you can't tell,' the man with the painted head said, 'he could have a couple of ribs broken clean and he wouldn't know till after.'

'Has he got a couple ribs broke?' Joe asked.

'God forbid,' Mr Kandinsky answered, 'God forbid.'

Blackie and Oliver must have told Shmule not to waste time, because he came out fast and made straight for the Python, who, being pleased with himself, was a bit careless. Shmule clasped his hands together and raised them for a rabbit punch, but he was too late. The Python crouched away, out of distance, not careless any more. Then a look of pain suddenly crossed Shmule's face, and the Python grinned and came in to attack, his hands low.

'He's hurt,' Sonia whispered.

'He's hurt all right,' the man in front of Joe said.

But what a surprise! Shmule suddenly leaped forward and caught the Python a great crack on the jaw with his left fist. The Python looked surprised and fell down.

'No boxing,' the crowd yelled.

The Python started to get up at once, but Shmule was on top of him, his knees to either side of his stomach, his hands firmly planted on his shoulders, pressing them to the canvas. As he pressed he strengthened the grip of his knees. The Python groaned, shouted. He jerked and jumped and twisted, but he couldn't throw Shmule off.

'He can give it,' the man said, 'but he can't take it. Go on, boy; do him!'

The Python beat the floor with both hands and Shmule let go at once.

'Good boy,' the man said.

'He should give him the same as he got,' Sonia said; 'why should he fight him clean?'

The crowd cheered Shmule, but the Python wasn't hurt as much as they thought, because as soon as Shmule broke away, he leaped to his feet. Not fast enough though. Shmule wasn't so green now. He didn't stop watching the Python for a second, and he saw him tensed to leap. Ready for him, he caught the Python another crack on the chin as he came up. The Python went down with Shmule on top of him, but he was saved by the bell.

'That's more like it,' the man said; 'he's got the old Python on the squirm, proper.'

'Get us some nuts, Fred,' the woman said.

'Fancy an ice?' the man asked.

'Some nuts, Fred,' the woman said again.

'How's the boy doing now, Sonia?' Mr Kandinsky asked.

'He's all right,' Sonia said; 'another round like that and he'll win.'

'We're winning,' Joe told his mother.

'That's good,' she replied. 'It's awful to see their faces.'

In the fourth round the Python set out to finish Shmule off. He tried all the fancy holds, the Indian death-lock, the flying mare, the cobra, but Shmule was like an eel; he didn't stay still long enough for the grips to take.

'He's using his speed now,' the man said; 'let's see the Python catch up with that.'

But the Python couldn't catch up with that. After a couple of minutes the crowd started to laugh, because the Python lumbered like a great ox, while Shmule danced circles round him, cracking him on the back and chest every so often. Now the Python was on his guard against face-blows, and being careful made him even more clumsy. He was furious with the crowd for laughing. He looked at Shmule through slit eyes wanting to murder him.

'Let me get my hands on you, laughing boy, that's all,' he growled.

Then suddenly Shmule nipped in close, his foot jabbed out, and the Python fell heavily on to the canvas, his arms round Shmule's leg. But as he fell Shmule struck the Python a heavy blow to the stomach, and pulled his leg free.

The Python held on to his stomach with both hands. His head came forward. His neck bent towards Shmule like a beast to the slaughterer.

Shmule folded his hands together as if to pray. He lifted them and carefully aiming, brought a rabbit punch with all his force clean on to the Python's neck. The Python slumped forward over his hands. Shmule stood back, watching. The Python didn't move.

'Cold meat!' someone shouted.

'Hammer!' all the tailors yelled.

'Hammer!' shouted Joe.

The Python was out cold.

IT was the latest night ever. It was late when Joe and his mother and Mr Kandinsky left Sonia at the swimming-baths waiting for Shmule, both of them to follow on later. It was late when they got home, but no one suggested that Joe should go to bed, because it was, after all, an occasion. Joe said it was only fair to bring Africana in, since he had been such a help, but Mr Kandinsky said, 'Leave him sleep. Tomorrow is also a day.'

Joe's mother lit the gas fire in the kitchen, and put the kettle on the stove to make a cup of tea. As they waited for the kettle Mr Kandinsky told them about the patent steam presser which, only four years old, he could buy for practically nothing from the Grosvenor Garment Company in Fournier Street. With a bit of patching up, tighten a few screws, a good re-padding job, scrape off the rust, a coat of paint, it would make a first-class presser, good as new.

Now Mr Kandinsky didn't have Shmule to worry about any more, he could concentrate on the steam presser again. In fact, now that Shmule had actually won the fight, it seemed unreasonable to Mr Kandinsky that he should't have the presser.

'A chance like this, Becky,' he said, 'doesn't, after all, come up every day. A chance of a lifetime. He would take thirty pound for it, he said, but I know better. He would be glad to get twenty pound as well. After all, all the big firms can buy new pressers, what do they want with an old machine four years old, rusty, dirty? And who's got thirty pounds who isn't a big firm? Believe me, he would be glad to take twenty. And yet who's got even twenty?'

'Shmule has got twenty-five pounds because you heard, the winner gets twenty-five pounds to himself,' Joe said.

Mr Kandinsky looked thunderstruck. He slapped his forehead with his palm. 'You're right, Joe,' he said.

'Shmule has got twenty-five pounds.'

Joe's mother looked over from the stove where she was pouring boiling water into the teapot.

'Shmule must buy Sonia a ring before anything else,' she said. 'It's a shame otherwise.'

'That's true,' Mr Kandinsky said, pursing his lips. 'Quite right. Mind you, if Shmule was to come along to me and tell me, "I bought the steam presser, what about a partnership?" I would tell him straightaway, "Certainly." But naturally Sonia must have a ring. Only this other way she wouldn't just be a girl with a ring marrying a young fellow, a worker in the tailoring. This way she is marrying a guvnor, a partner in a business, and what is more, a growing business. Because I tell you, Becky, with a patent steam presser we can take in so much jobbing, we can make a living from this alone. Still, Sonia must have a ring. Maybe it is the only chance Shmule gets his whole life, but it doesn't matter. A ring is important.'

Mr Kandinsky was very upset. It was selfish of Sonia to stop Shmule becoming a guvnor. Mr Kandinsky pressed the lemon in his glass with a spoon. Joe sipped his milk, wondering what Africana would do about this. Then they heard voices on the stairs.

Shmule and Sonia came in arm in arm. Though he looked tired, Shmule's eyes were bright.

'I couldn't get him away from there,' Sonia said. 'They all wanted to see him.'

Mr Kandinsky gripped Shmule's hand.

'Good luck to you always,' he said, 'good health, and every blessing.'

Joe's mother said, 'It was awful to watch, but you were marvellous, Shmule, marvellous. Only don't let him do it any more, Sonia. You mustn't do it any more, Shmule. Buy Sonia a ring now, and finish with the wrestling.'

'She's right,' Mr Kandinsky said. 'It's for the beast of the field.'

'You know what he told me round one?' Shmule said. 'He told me to lie down in the seventh, I could share the purse with him. That's what he told me.'

'That Python,' Sonia said, angry, 'he wanted Shmule to lie down.'

'When I tell him I am fighting clean he says he'll ruin me.'

'You hear?' Mr Kandinsky said to all of them. 'You hear what kind of a business this wrestling is?'

'It kills you for real development of the body beautiful,' Sonia said.

'No good for the muscular tone or the efficiency,' Shmule said. 'Still, I can give baby a ring.'

Sonia hugged him.

'I want to talk to you with a serious proposition,' Mr Kandinsky said, clearing his throat and holding his hand up for silence. 'Namely, now that you got a bit of capital, and I am, after all, the truth is the truth, an old man. Namely, a partnership deal.'

Shmule looked more dazed than the dreaded Python the last time he was hit. Sonia hugged him again.

'Baby,' she said, 'you hear?'

'But,' continued Mr Kandinsky, and he explained that Shmule would have to bring with him a patent steam presser.

'Thank you very much,' said Shmule, 'for a hundred eighty-seven pounds a patent presser. Not two?'

'Don't grab,' Mr Kandinsky said; 'listen a minute.' He told him about the second-hand presser over at Grosvenor Garments.

'You think he would take twenty?' Shmule asked, stroking his lip.

'Take?' answered Mr Kandinsky. 'He would drag it out of your hands.'

Sonia didn't say anything. Her face couldn't make up its mind whether she was pleased or not. It was a difficult decision.

'Let me speak to Sonia a minute,' Mr Kandinsky said. 'Sonia,' he said, 'here you are a young woman in the bloom of her beauty, a perfect mate for life with this Maccabaeus here.'

Sonia blushed and looked at Shmule.

'Two years you have been patient,' Mr Kandinsky continued. 'Listen, Sonia. This is important. Two years you have lived on the word of this man alone. No ring to bind the promise, so that sometimes other people, busy-bodies with big mouths, who didn't know what kind of girl you are, they said, "Look, at Sonia, no ring. What kind of an engagement?" ' Mr Kandinsky paused.

Sonia's eyes were full of tears as she listened. It was no more than the truth. She had been marvellous, it was true.

Mr Kandinsky continued. 'Sonia,' he said, 'they didn't know this boy, what a fighter he is, how clean and honest, and what a worker, no one to touch him in the entire East End. Him they saw tonight. Now they know what he is. And you saw him, too, what he will do for you, to get you a better ring than any girl in Novak Blouses ever had.'

'Gay-day Blouses,' Sonia said tenderly.

'Gay-day,' Mr Kandinsky repeated. 'But something else no girl in Gay-day ever had. You know what it is?' He pointed to Sonia to answer the question. She shook her head.

'They didn't marry a fellow who was, already, so young, a guvnor in his own business. That's what they didn't have.'

Mr Kandinsky made his last point in a loud voice, his pointing finger sweeping round the whole world to find another girl who could say she had done better than Sonia.

'Now, Sonia,' he continued after a moment in which Sonia squeezed Shmule's hand. 'I ask you straight out. Which is better, such a husband, a champion, a guvnor, with the world in front of him; or a fiancé, works for Kandinsky, the Fashion Street trousers-maker, wrestles Saturday nights to make a few pounds, he might be able to get married one day to a girl at Gay-day Blouses with a big diamond ring? Don't answer me,' he went on as Sonia opened her mouth. 'Think first. It is in your hands, his life, your life; I don't want to influence you. Drink a cup of tea and think.'

That was how Mr Kandinsky made Shmule his partner, and though everyone was pleased, they said Joe should be in bed.

THE next morning was fine and sunny. When Joe woke up he heard the horses clopping over the cobbles, and goods-trains rattling from the arches. The first thing he thought was he must tell Africana. He dressed quietly, and leaving his mother to have her Sunday morning lie-in, ran downstairs.

Mr Kandinsky was already at work, and Joe shouted good morning and rushed into the yard.

'Good old unicorn!' he shouted out to Africana, but there was no rustle from Africana's house. The house looked like a pile of old boxes waiting to be chopped up for fire-wood, desolate. Africana was gone.

'He's gone,' Joe shouted, running back to the work-room. 'He's gone, Mr Kandinsky, he's gone.'

'What?' said Mr Kandinsky. 'Who's gone?'

'Africana's gone, he's just gone,' Joe cried, and how would he ever bring his father back from Africa?

'Let's have a look,' Mr Kandinsky said. 'Let's keep our head and look.'

They searched the yard carefully.

'Let's look in the house again,' Mr Kandinsky said.

'It's empty,' Joe replied, tears coming fast. 'Can't you see, it's empty?'

'Let's look, all the same,' said Mr Kandinsky.

He searched through the bed of remnants.

'What's this?' he said. He bent down and picked up something. It was a gleaming golden sovereign. He handed it to Joe.

'What is it?' asked Joe.

'Come inside, Joe,' Mr Kandinsky said. 'I will tell you.'

'He's gone,' Joe said, the tears still there.

'Come inside,' said Mr Kandinsky, and he put his arm round Joe's shoulder.

'You know what this is, Joe?' he asked, giving him the sovereign. 'This is a golden sovereign. And what has happened is plain as my nose. You could see yourself that unicorn didn't do so well in Fashion Street, ailing the whole time, no interest, miserable the whole day. So you know what he's done? He's gone back to Africa like you said he should. But just to show it's nothing personal, he left this golden sovereign on account of that magic horn worth five thousand pound.'

'Ten thousand,' said Joe.

'Ten thousand pound, I mean,' continued Mr Kandinsky. 'Meanwhile, keep this for luck.'

'He won't come back,' Joe said.

'Maybe not,' Mr Kandinsky replied. 'Unicorns can't grow in Fashion Street, but boys have to.'

Joe went upstairs slowly, rubbing the golden sovereign between his fingers. There was a small rough piece broken on top of it, but otherwise it was like the coin on Mr Kandinsky's father's watch-chain, which made two golden sovereigns in the house.

When his mother came into the kitchen, her face blanched with sleep, Joe asked whether two sovereigns would bring his father back. It was the only thing the unicorn had forgotten to arrange. With the sleep still on her, she didn't know at first what he meant. After Joe explained carefully, she said yes, it was a great help, and they would find his father's return passage money some-how. They would never go to Africa, it was a dream, but he would come back to them, he would come back soon. Next week she must see about Joe starting school. He was growing up learning nothing about life.

Joe rolled the sovereign on the table thinking that if all the pets he had ever had were in the yard now, he could charge people pennies to come in. They would cheer and throw more pennies when they saw Africana's shining horn stretching high above the slate rooftops.

After breakfast he went into the yard to play, although he had no special game in mind. For a little while he missed Africana, but soon he thought of something. In the end, it brought him safely to Africa.

ALSO AVAILABLE IN THE SERIES

FRANK BAKER

MISS HARGREAVES

When, on the spur of a moment, Norman Huntley and his friend Henry invent an eighty-three year-old woman called Miss Hargreaves, they are inspired to post a letter to their new fictional friend. It is only meant to be a silly, harmless game—until Miss Hargreaves arrives on their doorstep. She is, to Norman's utter disbelief, exactly as he had imagined her: enchanting, eccentric, and endlessly astounding. He hadn't imagined, however, how much havoc an imaginary octogenarian could wreak in his sleepy Buckinghamshire home town.

*

"A fantasy of the most hilarious description—the kind of novel, I fancy, that is badly wanted at the moment, and its central idea is one which has rarely, if, indeed, ever, been used before."
—*SUNDAY TIMES* (UK)

"Having met Miss Hargreaves, you won't want to be long out of her company—Frank Baker's novel is witty, joyful, and moving but above all an extraordinary work of the imagination."
—STUCK-IN-A-BOOK.BLOGSPOT.COM

*

ISBN: 978-1-60819-051-5 · PAPERBACK · U.S. $14.00

BLOOMSBURY

COMING SOON

RACHEL FERGUSON

THE BRONTËS WENT TO WOOLWORTHS

Meet the Carne sisters, Deirdre, Katrine, and Sheil, growing up together in 1930s London. Eldest sister Deirdre is a journalist, Katrine a fledgling actress, and young Sheil is still with her governess; together they live a life unchecked by their mother in their bohemian town house. Irrepressibly imaginative, the sisters cannot resist making up stories, as they have since childhood; from their talking nursery toys, Ironface the Doll and Dion Saffyn the pierrot, to their fulsomely imagined friendship with real high-court Judge Toddington—whom, since Mrs. Carne's jury duty, they have affectionately called Toddy. But when Deirdre meets Toddy's real-life wife at a charity bazaar, the sisters are forced to confront the subject of their imaginings—and this may mean the end of their childish innocence.

✳

"Marvellously successful."
—A.S BYATT

"The family at its most eccentric and bohemian – a pure concoction of wonderful invention. What an extraordinary meeting I have just had with the Carnes."
—DOVEGREYREADER.TYPEPAD.COM

✳

ISBN: 978-1-60819-053-9 · PAPERBACK · U.S. $14.00

BLOOMSBURY

COMING SOON

ADA LEVERSON
LOVE'S SHADOW

This first novel by Ada Leverson (whom Oscar Wilde called "the wittiest woman in the world") is the story of Edith and Bruce Ottley, who live in a very new, very small, very white flat in Knightsbridge. On the surface they are like every other respectable couple in Edwardian London, and that is precisely why Edith is beginning to feel a little bored. Excitement comes in the form of the dazzling and glamorous Hyacinth Verney, who doesn't understand why Edith is married to one of the greatest bores in society. But then, Hyacinth doesn't really understand any of the courtships, jealousies, and love affairs of their coterie: why the dashing Cecil Reeve insists on being so elusive, why her loyal friend Anne is so stubbornly content with being a spinster, and why she just can't seem to take her mind off love…

✳

"Saki meets Jane Austen in the delectable Edwardian comedies of Ada Leverson.
A great discovery awaits her new readers."
—BARRY HUMPHRIES

"A perceptive, witty and wise portrayal of an ill-assorted marriage
and unrequited love."
—RANDOMJOTTINGS.TYPEPAD.COM

✳

ISBN: 978-1-60819-050-8 · PAPERBACK · U.S. $14.00

BLOOMSBURY

COMING SOON

JOYCE DENNYS

HENRIETTA'S WAR

NEWS FROM THE HOME FRONT 1939–1942

Spirited Henrietta wishes she was the kind of doctor's wife who knew exactly how to deal with the daily upheavals of war. But then, everyone in her close-knit Devonshire village seems to find different ways to cope: There's the indomitable Lady B, who writes to Hitler every night to tell him precisely what she thinks of him; the terrifyingly efficient Mrs. Savernack, who relishes the opportunity to sit on umpteen committees and boss everyone around; flighty, flirtatious Faith, who is utterly preoccupied with the latest hats and flashing her shapely legs; and Charles, Henrietta's hardworking husband, who manages to sleep through a bomb landing in their neighbor's garden. With life turned upside down under the shadow of war, Henrietta chronicles the dramas, squabbles, and loyal friendships that unfold in her affectionate letters to her "dear childhood friend" Robert.

Leavened by witty line illustrations, this novel makes a wry and moving portrait of London during World War II.

*

"Wonderfully evocative of English middle-class life at the time ...
never fails to cheer me up."
—SUSAN HILL, *GOOD HOUSEKEEPING* (UK)

"Warm and funny, but candid and telling too. A real delight!"
—CORNFLOWER.TYPEPAD.COM

*

ISBN: 978-1-60819-049-2 · PAPERBACK · U.S. $14.00

BLOOMSBURY

COMING SOON

D. E. STEVENSON
MRS. TIM OF THE REGIMENT

Originally the first in a popular series of four Mrs. Tim novels, this mischievous book tells the story of Hester Christie, the husband of Tim, a military man. When Tim gets stationed far away, Mrs. Tim is busy with more responsibilities than she can handle—domestic chores, social obligations, and parenting, to name just a few. She decides to write diaries of her daily events, as a means of gaining control of her life. Now, all her mischief and curiosity is recorded. All may seem innocent until a certain Major Morley turns up and begins to court her while her husband is away.

✳

"The writer's unflagging humour, her shrewd, worldly wisdom, and
her extremely realistic pictures of garrison life make it all good reading."
—*TIMES LITERARY SUPPLEMENT* (UK)

"Delightful domestic comedy."
—FRISBEEWIND.BLOGSPOT.COM

✳

ISBN: 978-1-60819-052-2 · PAPERBACK · U.S. $14.00

BLOOMSBURY

The History of Bloomsbury Publishing

Bloomsbury Publishing was founded in 1986 to publish books of excellence and originality. Its authors include Margaret Atwood, John Berger, William Boyd, David Guterson, Khaled Hosseini, John Irving, Anne Michaels, Michael Ondaatje, J.K. Rowling, Donna Tartt and Barbara Trapido. Its logo is Diana, the Roman Goddess of Hunting.

In 1994 Bloomsbury floated on the London Stock Exchange and added both a paperback and a children's list. Bloomsbury is based in Soho Square in London and expanded to New York in 1998 and Berlin in 2003. In 2000 Bloomsbury acquired A&C Black and now publishes *Who's Who, Whitaker's Almanack, Wisden Cricketers' Almanack* and the *Writers' & Artists' Yearbook*. Many books, bestsellers and literary awards later, Bloomsbury is one of the world's leading independent publishing houses.

Launched in 2009, The Bloomsbury Group continues the company's tradition of publishing books with perennial, word-of-mouth appeal. This series celebrates lost classics written by both men and women from the early twentieth century, books recommended by readers for readers. Literary bloggers, authors, friends and colleagues have shared their suggestions of cherished books worthy of revival. To send in your recommendation, please write to:

The Bloomsbury Group
Bloomsbury USA
175 Fifth Ave
New York, NY 10010
Or e-mail: info@bloomsburyusa.com

For more information on all titles in The Bloomsbury Group series and to submit your recommendations online please visit www.bloomsbury.com/thebloomsburygroup

For more information on all Bloomsbury authors and for all the latest news please visit www.bloomsburyusa.com